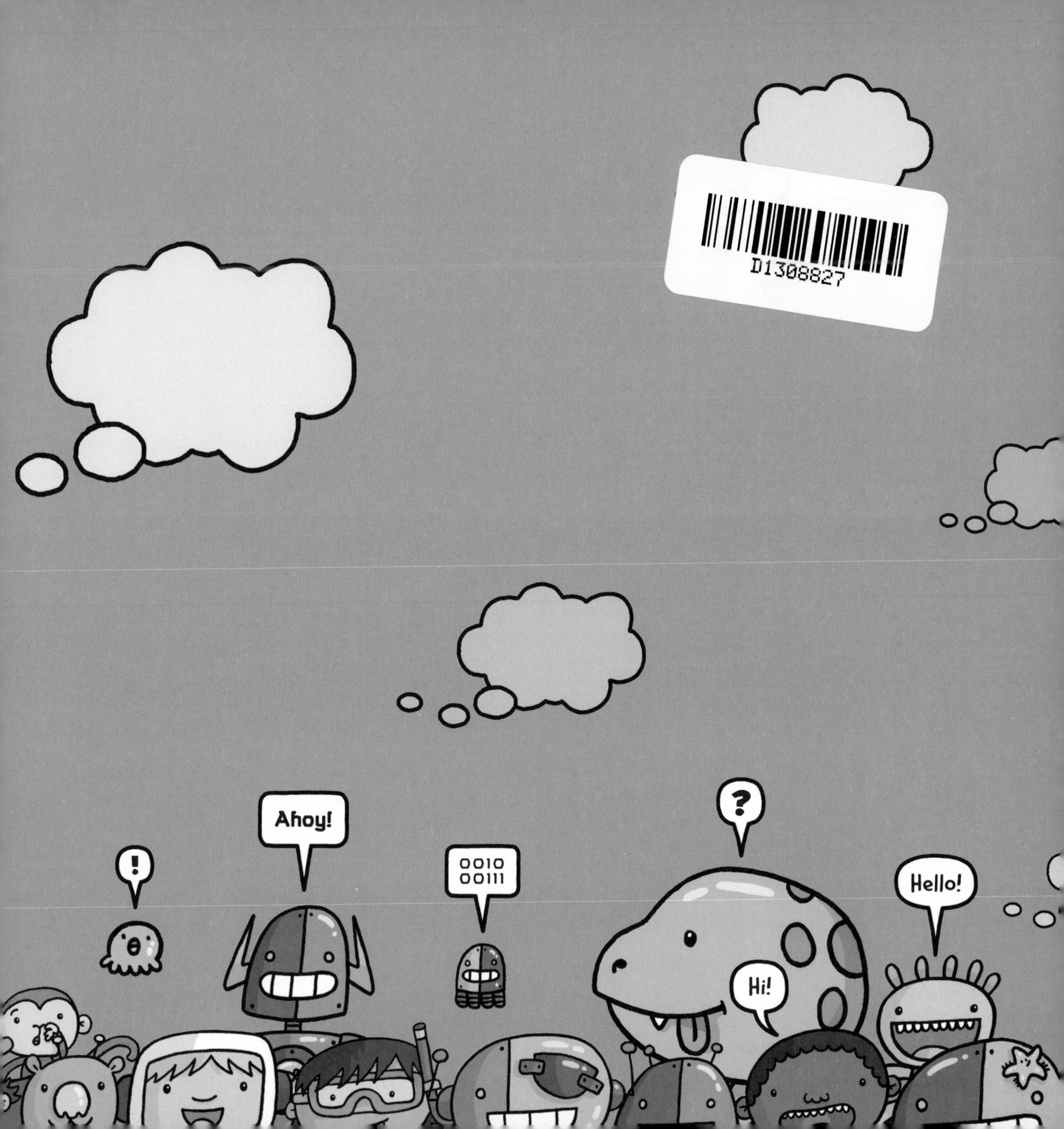

!
Ahoy!
0010
00111
?
Hello!
Hi!

COMICS LAND

by
CAPSTONE

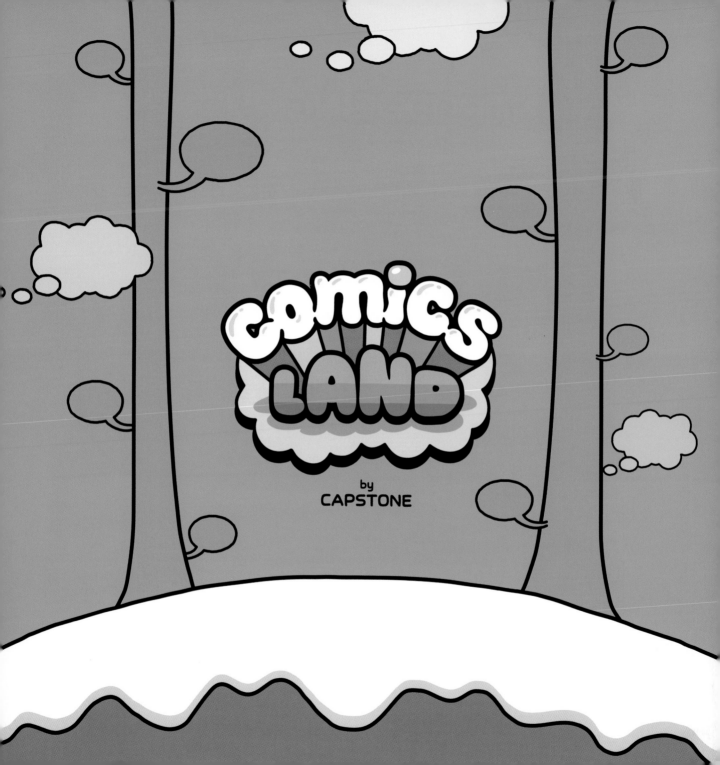

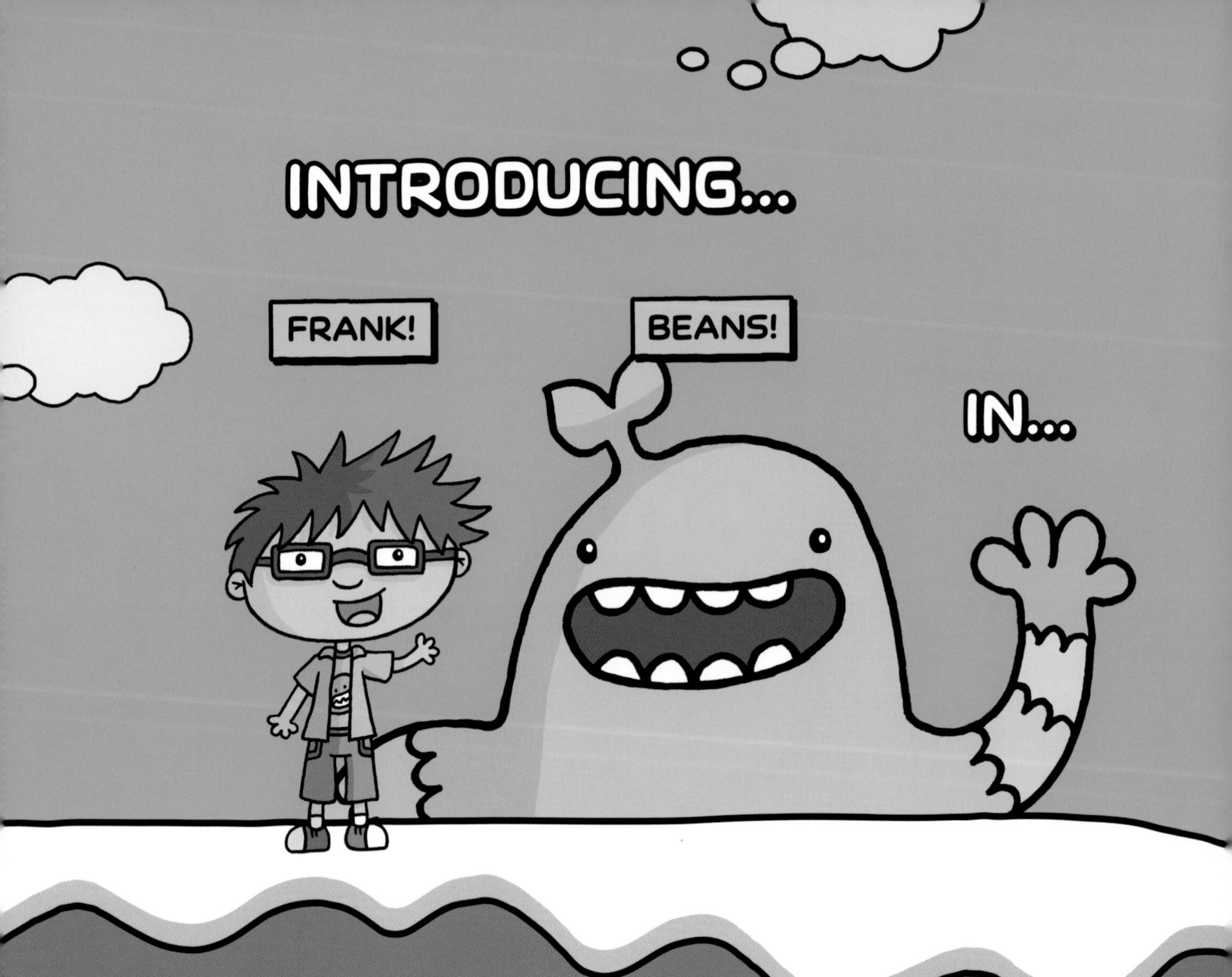
INTRODUCING...
FRANK!
BEANS!
IN...

capstone
www.capstoneyoungreaders.com

1710 Roe Crest Drive, North Mankato, Minnesota 56003

Cataloging-in-Publication data is available on the Library of Congress website.
ISBN: 978-1-4342-6284-4 (hardcover) · ISBN: 978-1-4342-4988-3 (library binding)
ISBN: 978-1-4342-6431-2 (eBook)

Printed in China by Nordica. 1213/CA21302220 112013 007892R

FRANK 'N' BEANS

written by
AMY & DONALD LEMKE

illustrated by
JESS BRADLEY

designed by
BOB LENTZ

edited by
JULIE GASSMAN

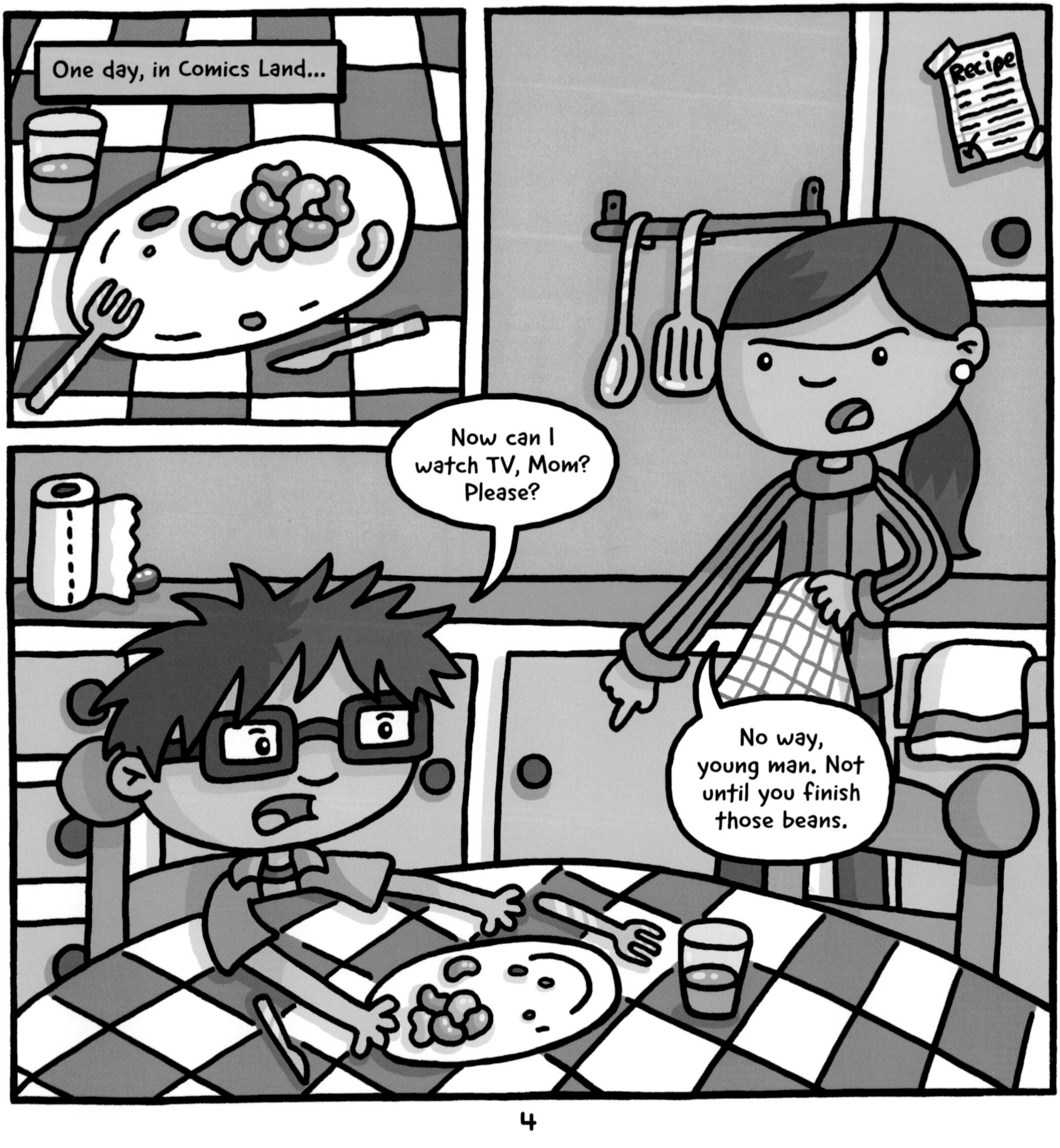
One day, in Comics Land...
Recipe
Now can I watch TV, Mom? Please?
No way, young man. Not until you finish those beans.

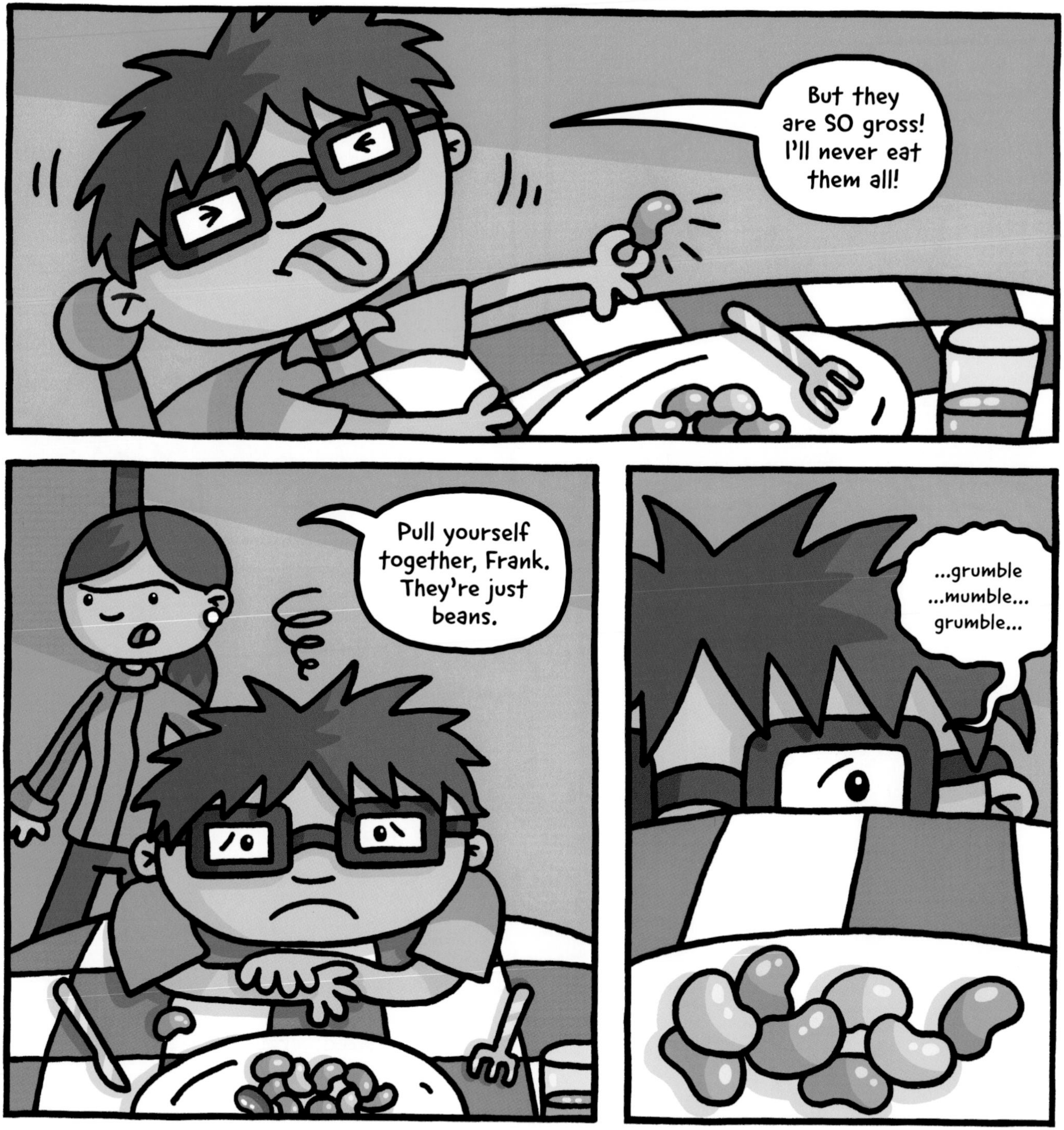
But they are SO gross! I'll never eat them all!
Pull yourself together, Frank. They're just beans.
...grumble ...mumble... grumble...

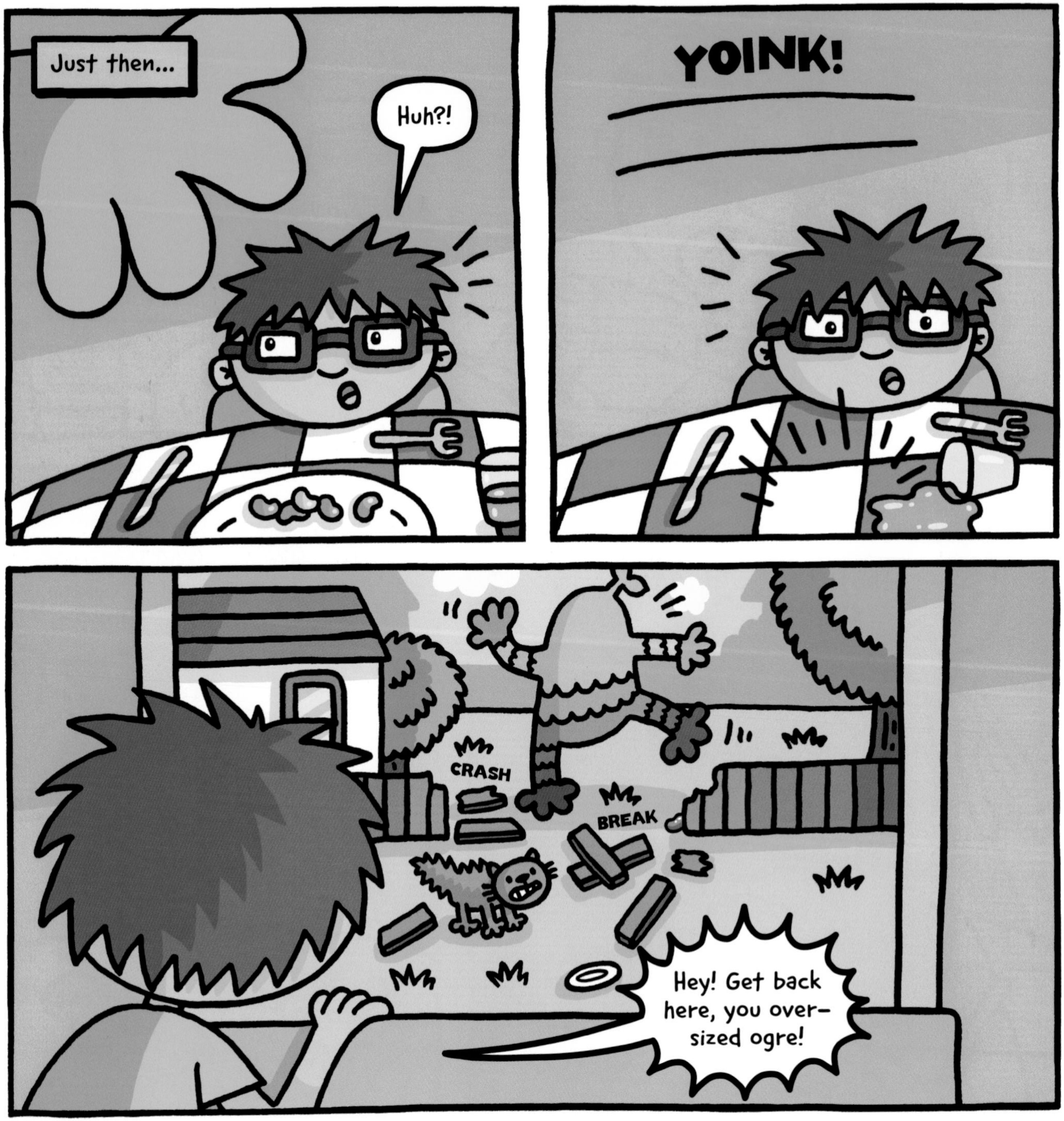

Just then...
Huh?!
YOINK!
CRASH
BREAK
Hey! Get back here, you over-sized ogre!

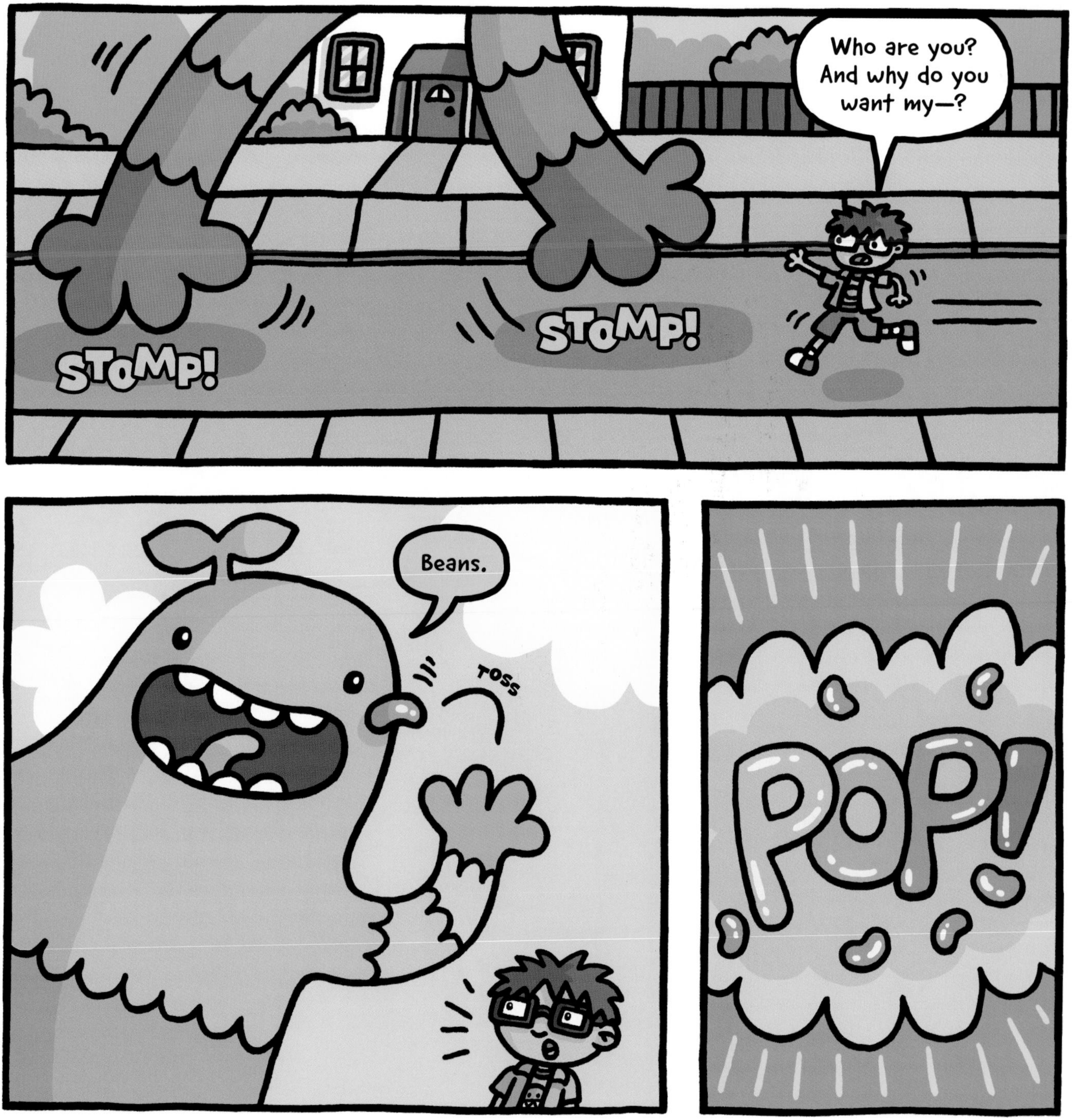
STOMP!
STOMP!
Who are you? And why do you want my—?
Beans.
TOSS
POP!

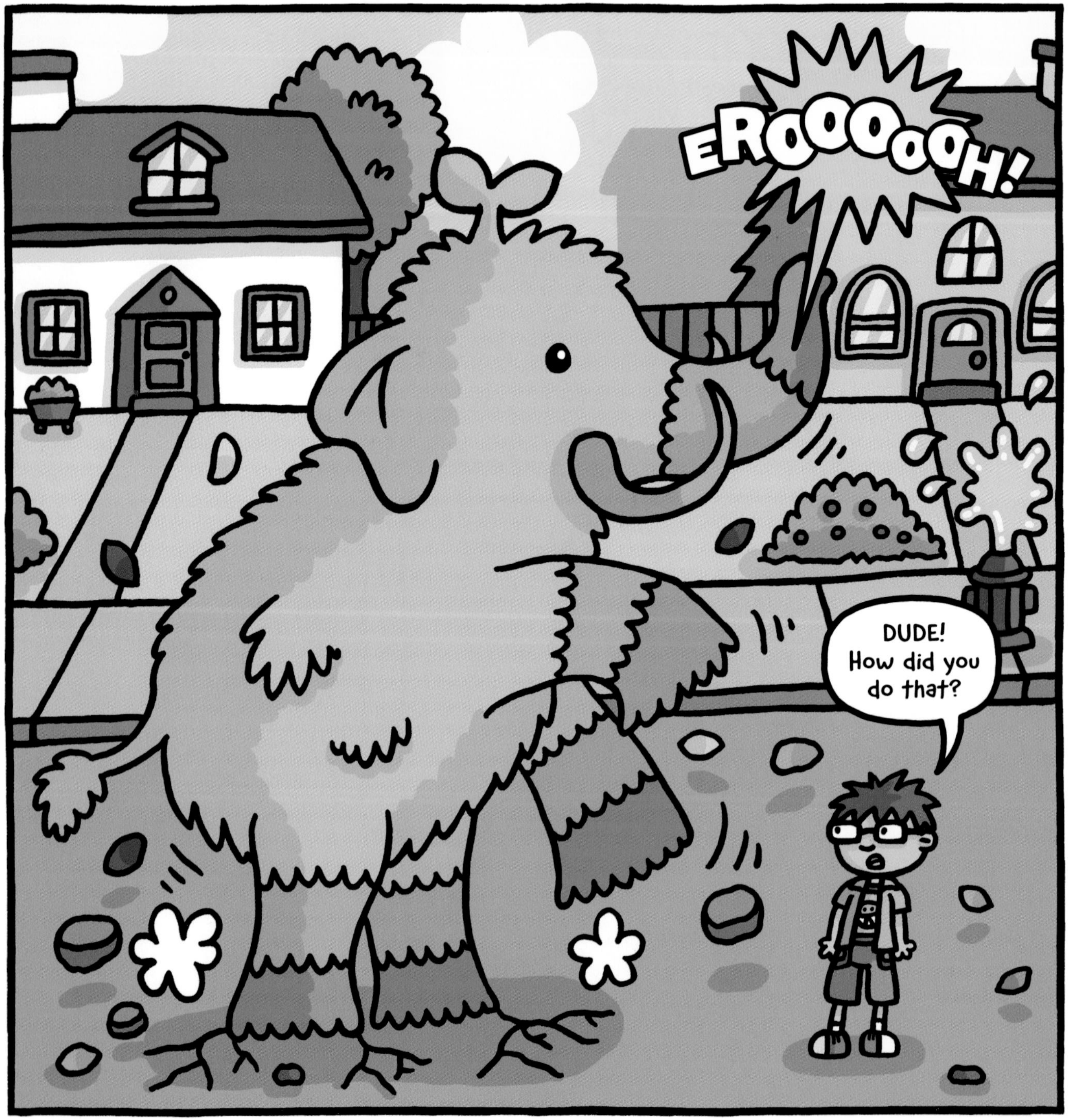
EROOOOOOH!
DUDE! How did you do that?

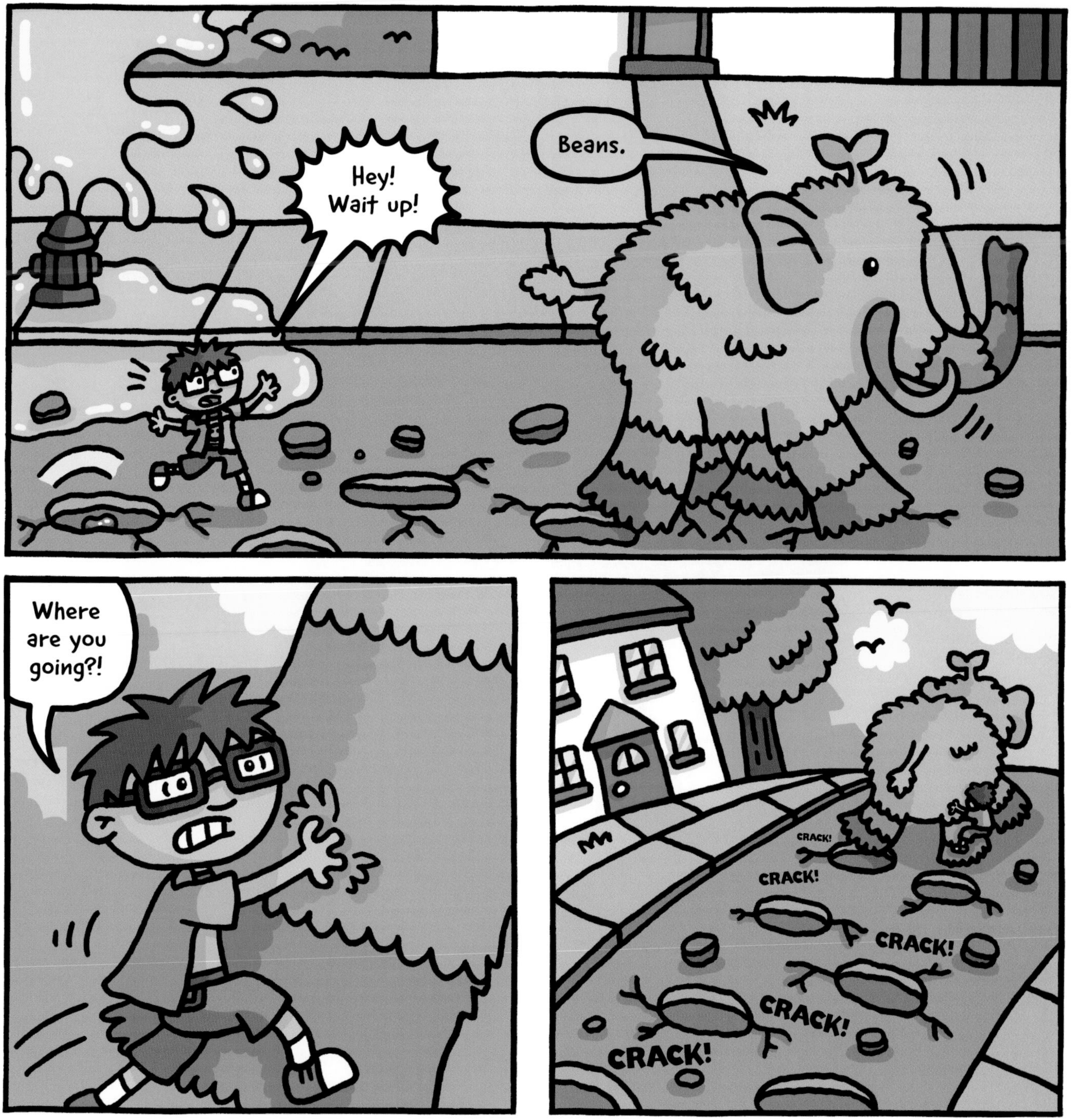
Hey! Wait up!
Beans.
Where are you going?!
CRACK!
CRACK!
CRACK!
CRACK!
CRACK!

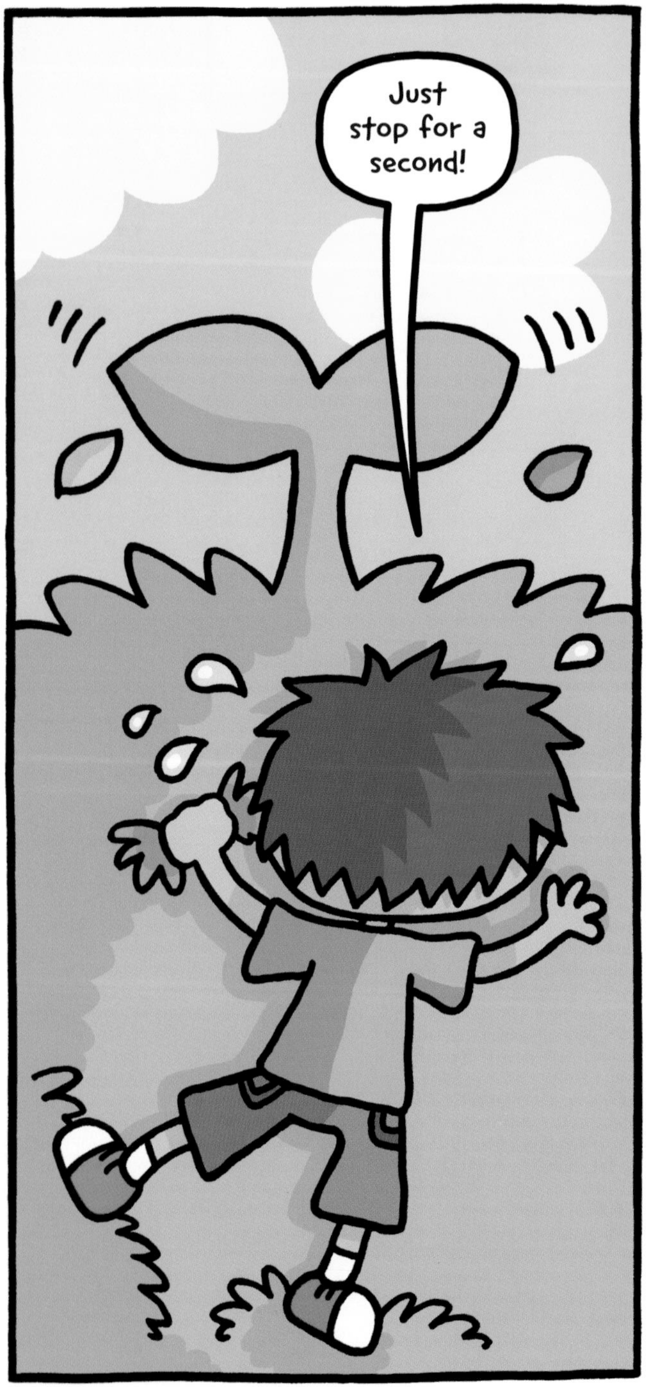
Just stop for a second!

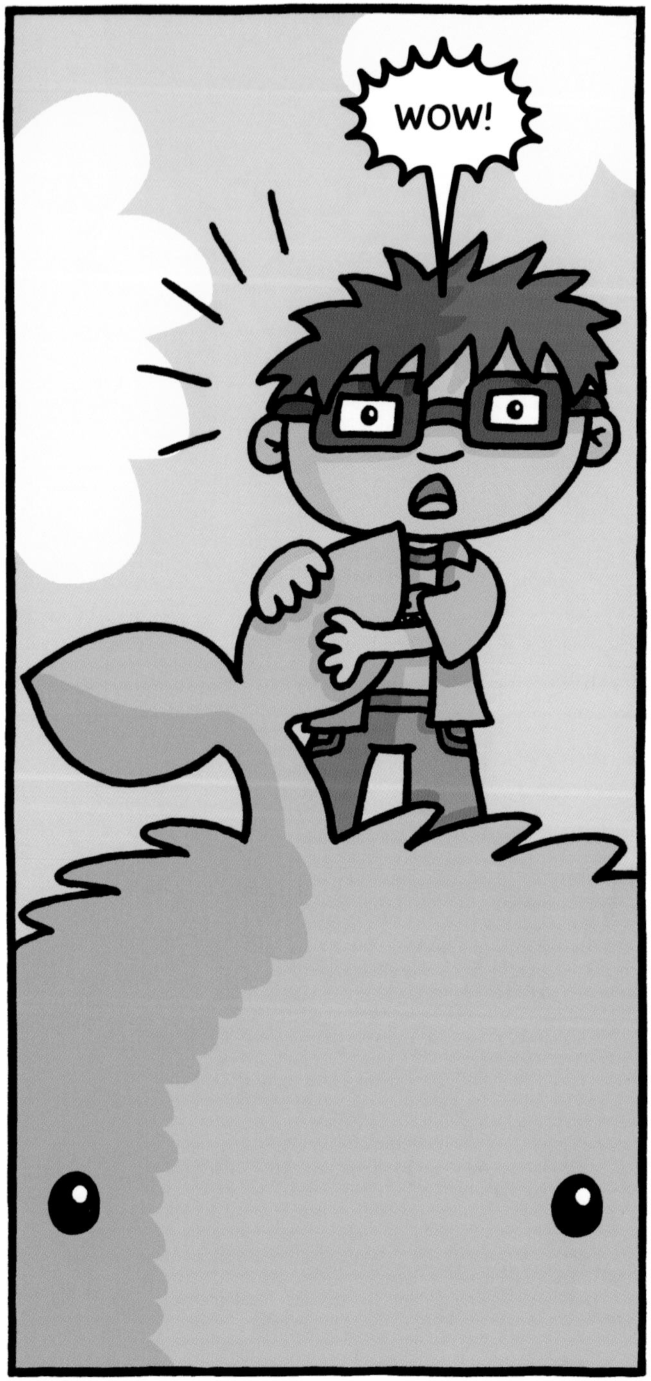
WOW!

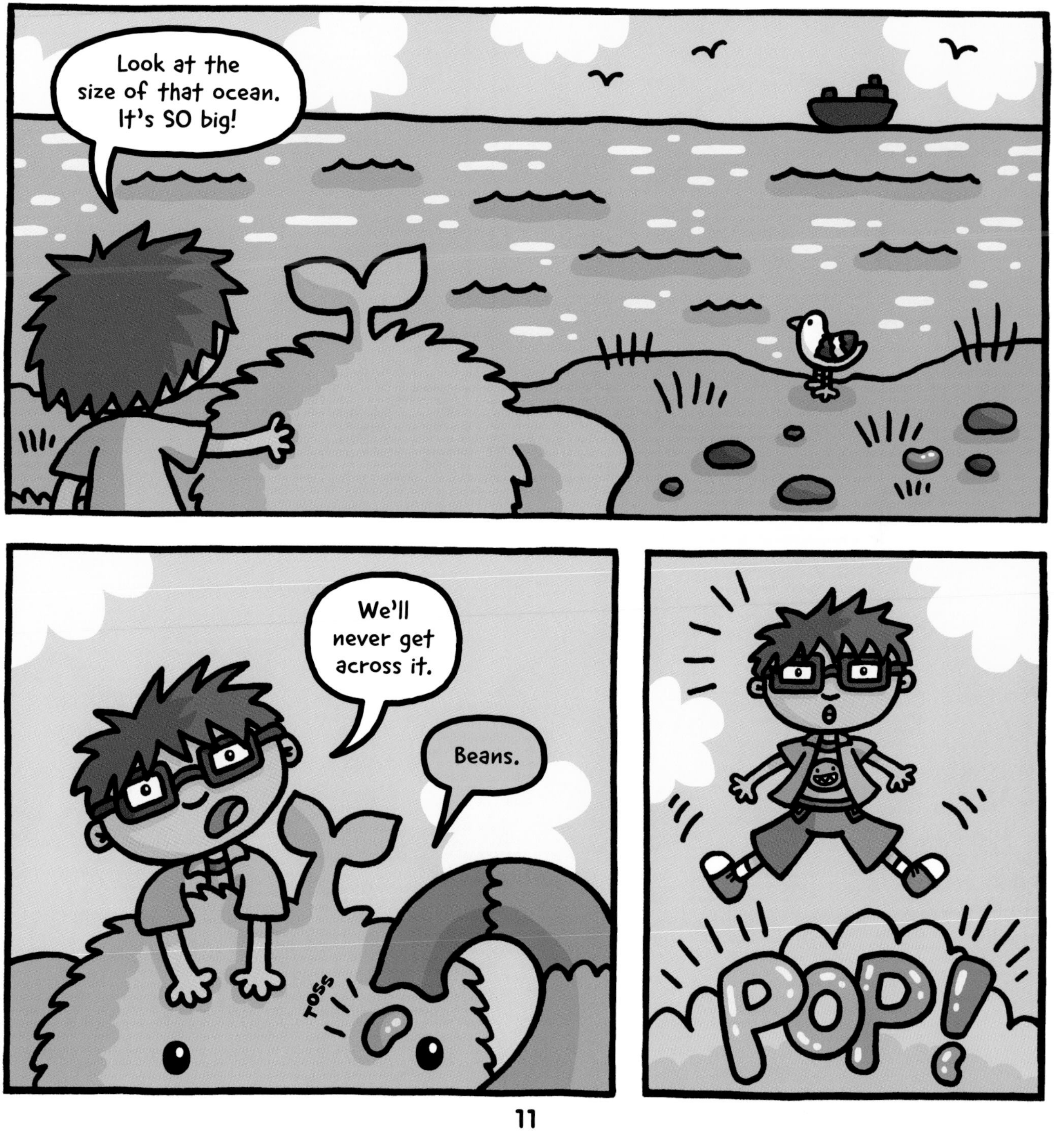
Look at the size of that ocean. It's SO big!
We'll never get across it.
Beans.
TOSS
POP!

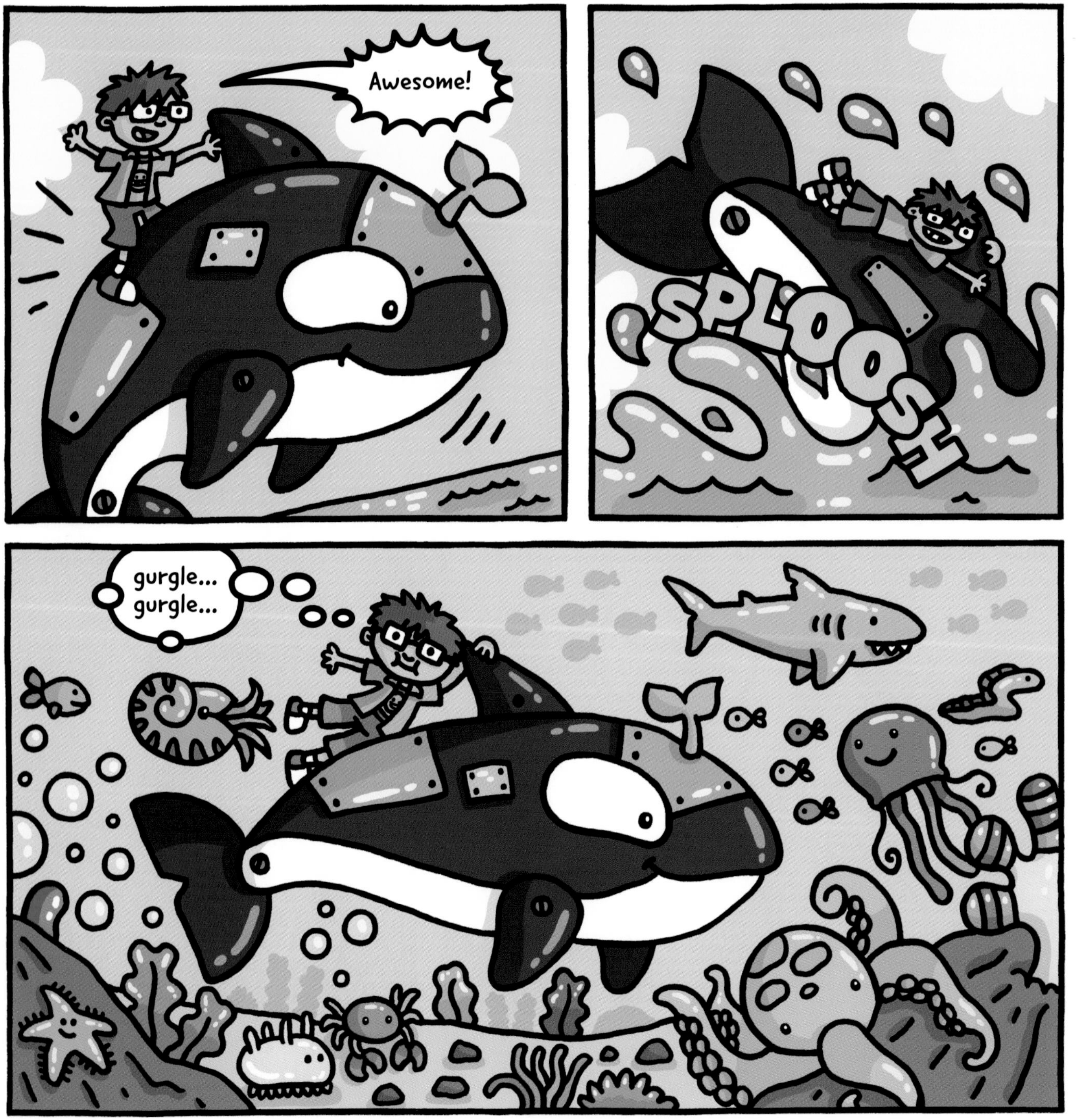
Awesome!
SPLOOSH
gurgle... gurgle...

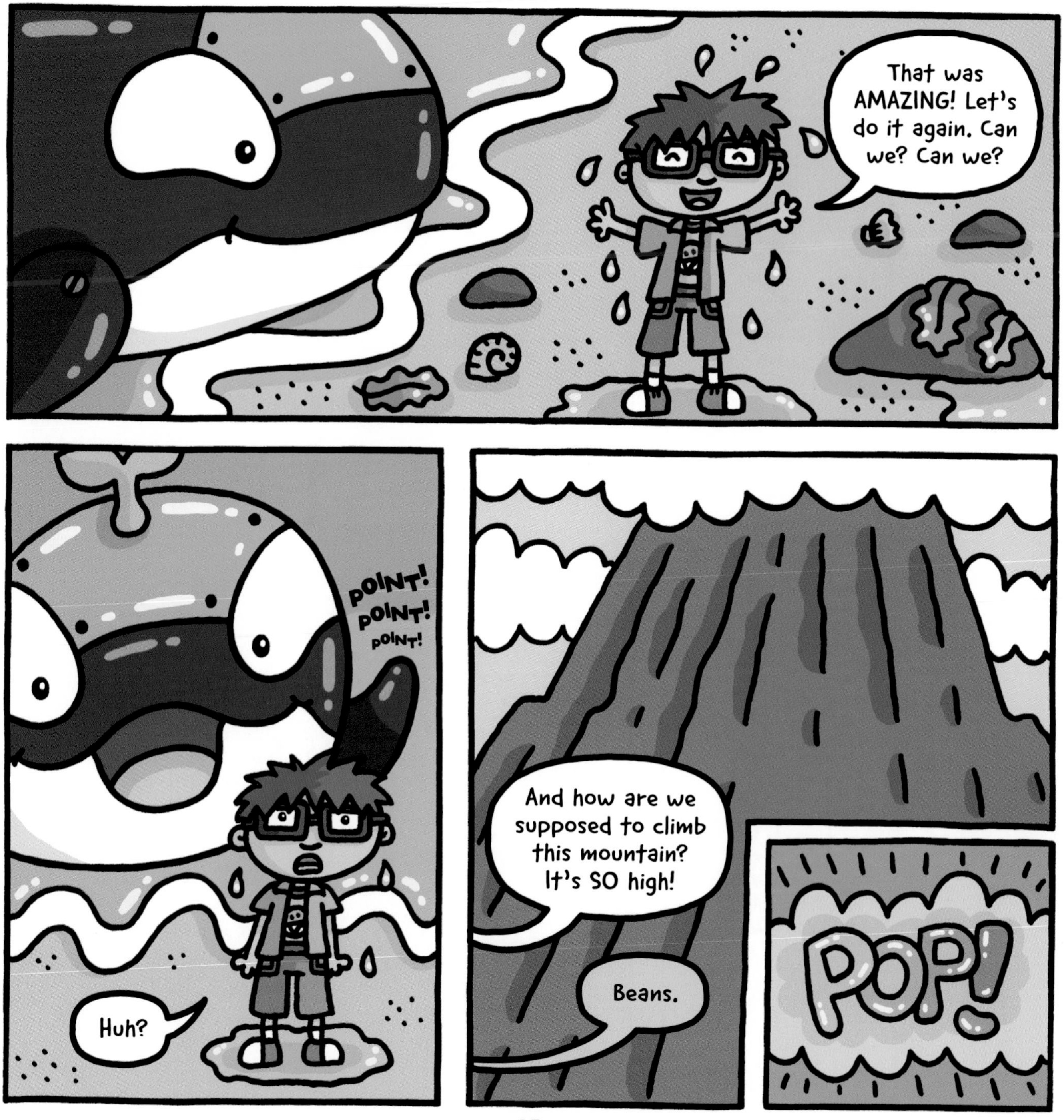
That was AMAZING! Let's do it again. Can we? Can we?
POINT! POINT! POINT!
Huh?
And how are we supposed to climb this mountain? It's SO high!
Beans.
POP!

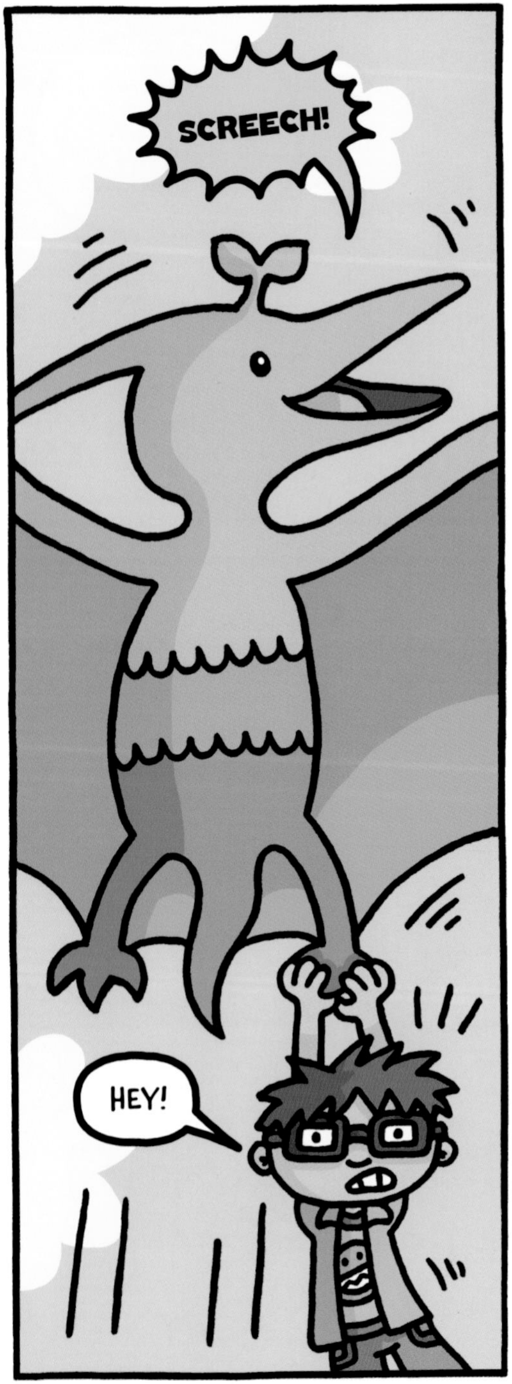
SCREECH!
HEY!

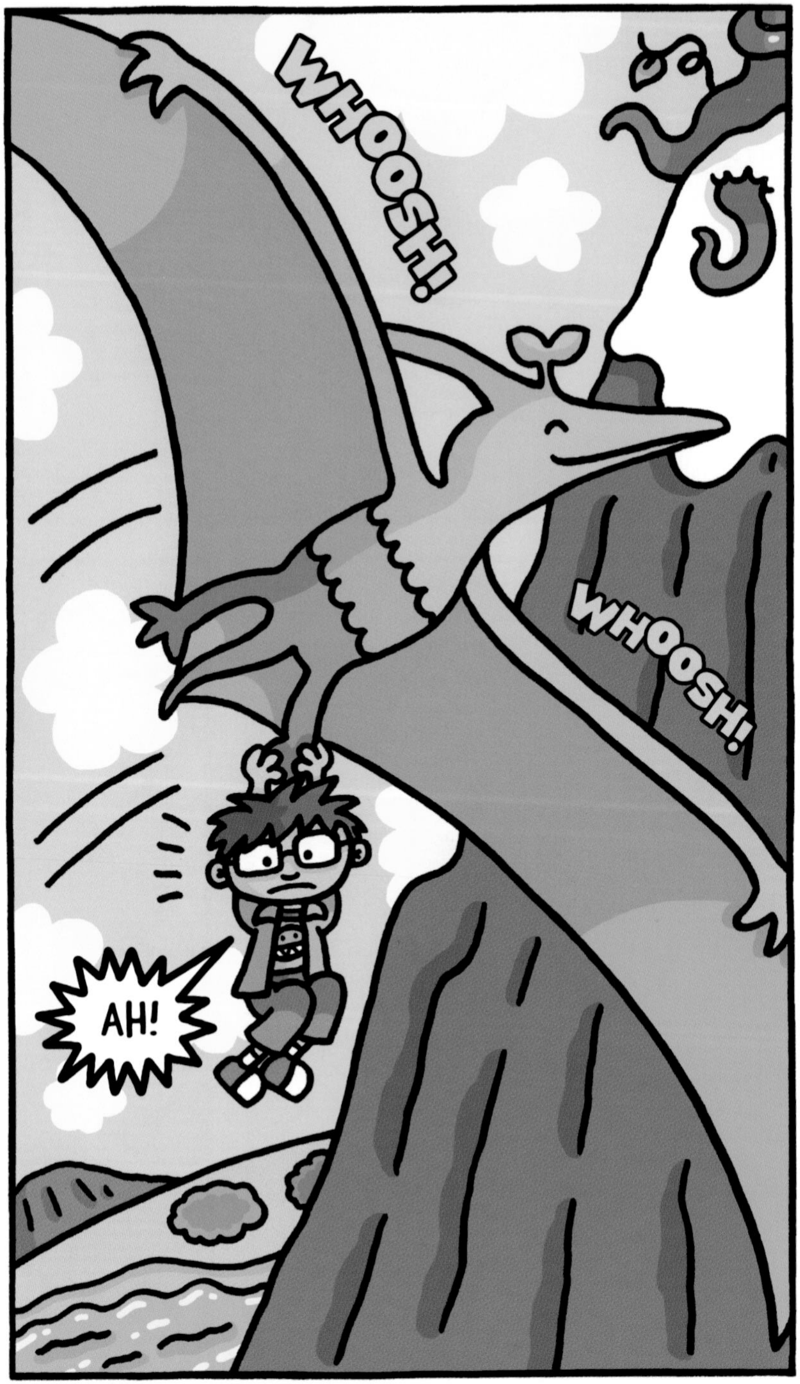
WHOOSH!
WHOOSH!
AH!

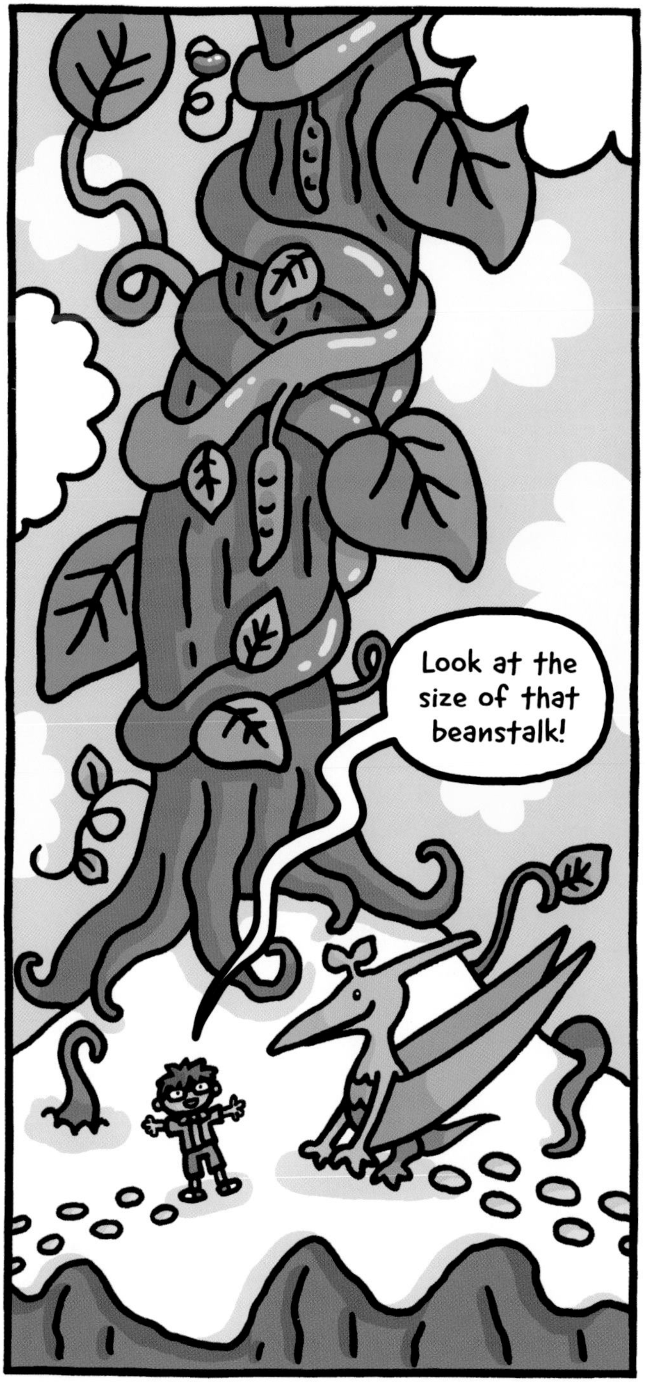
Look at the size of that beanstalk!

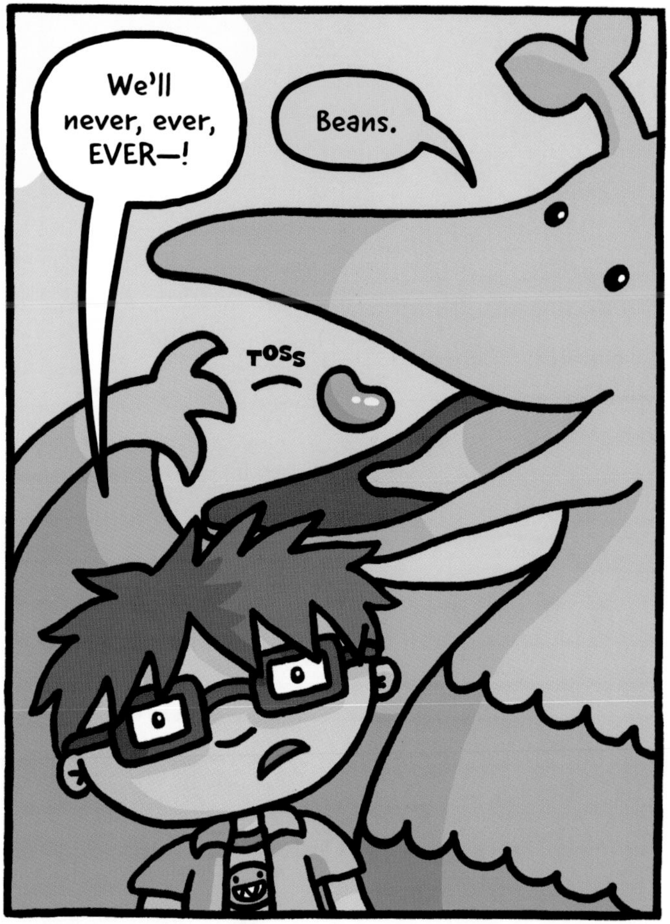
We'll never, ever, EVER—!
Beans.
TOSS

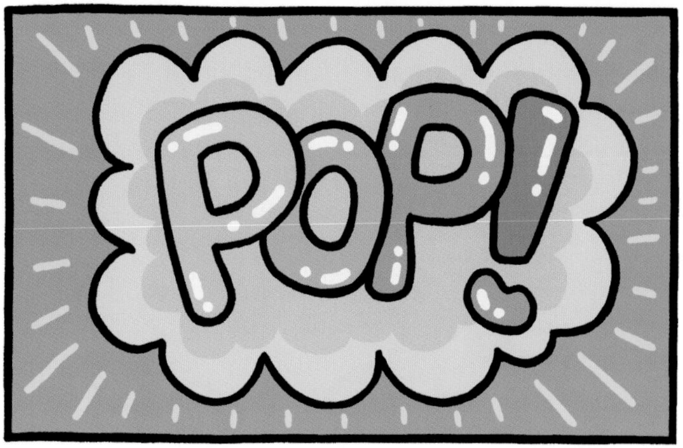
POP!

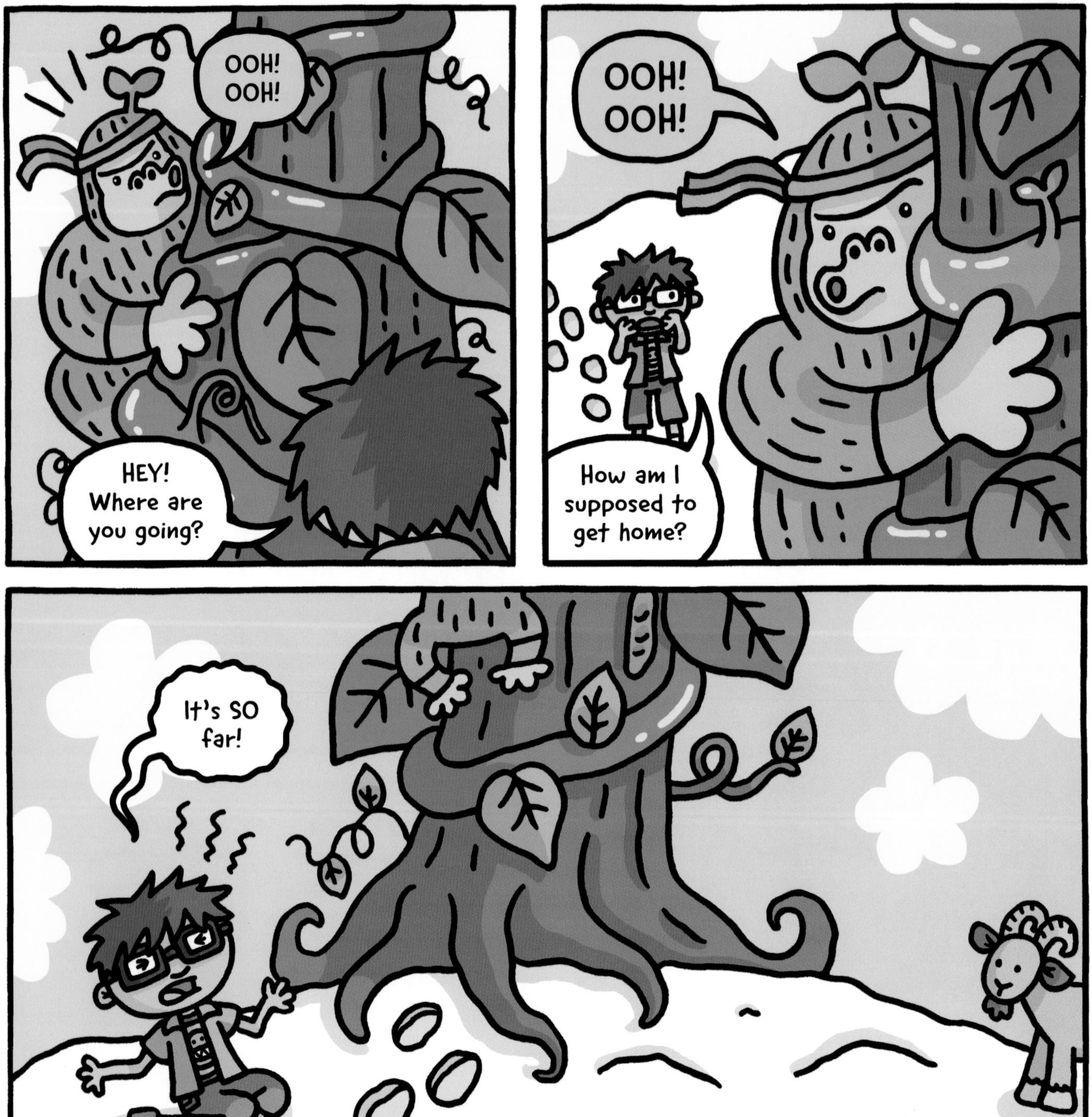
OOH! OOH!
HEY! Where are you going?
OOH! OOH!
How am I supposed to get home?
It's SO far!

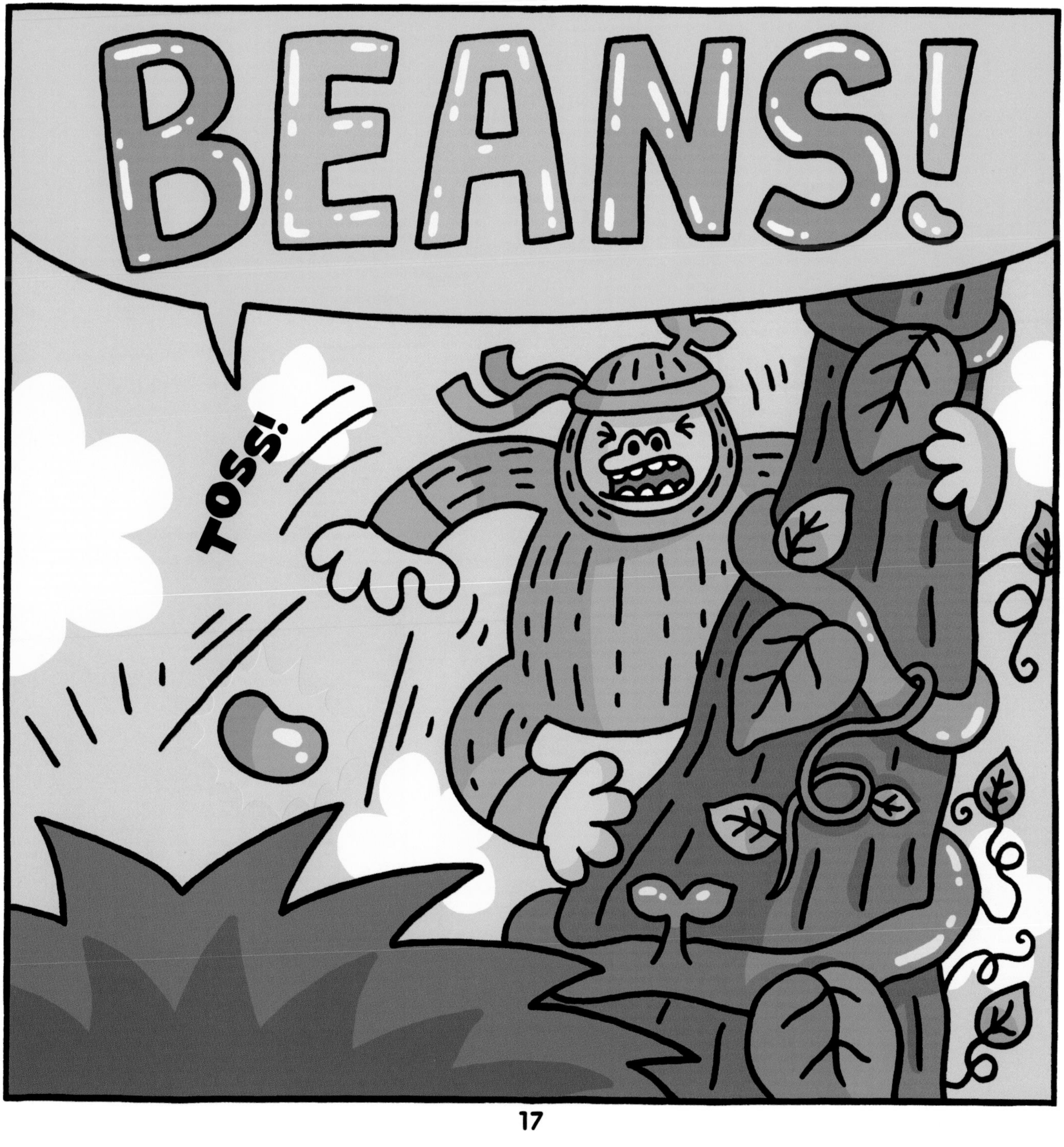
BEANS!
TOSS!

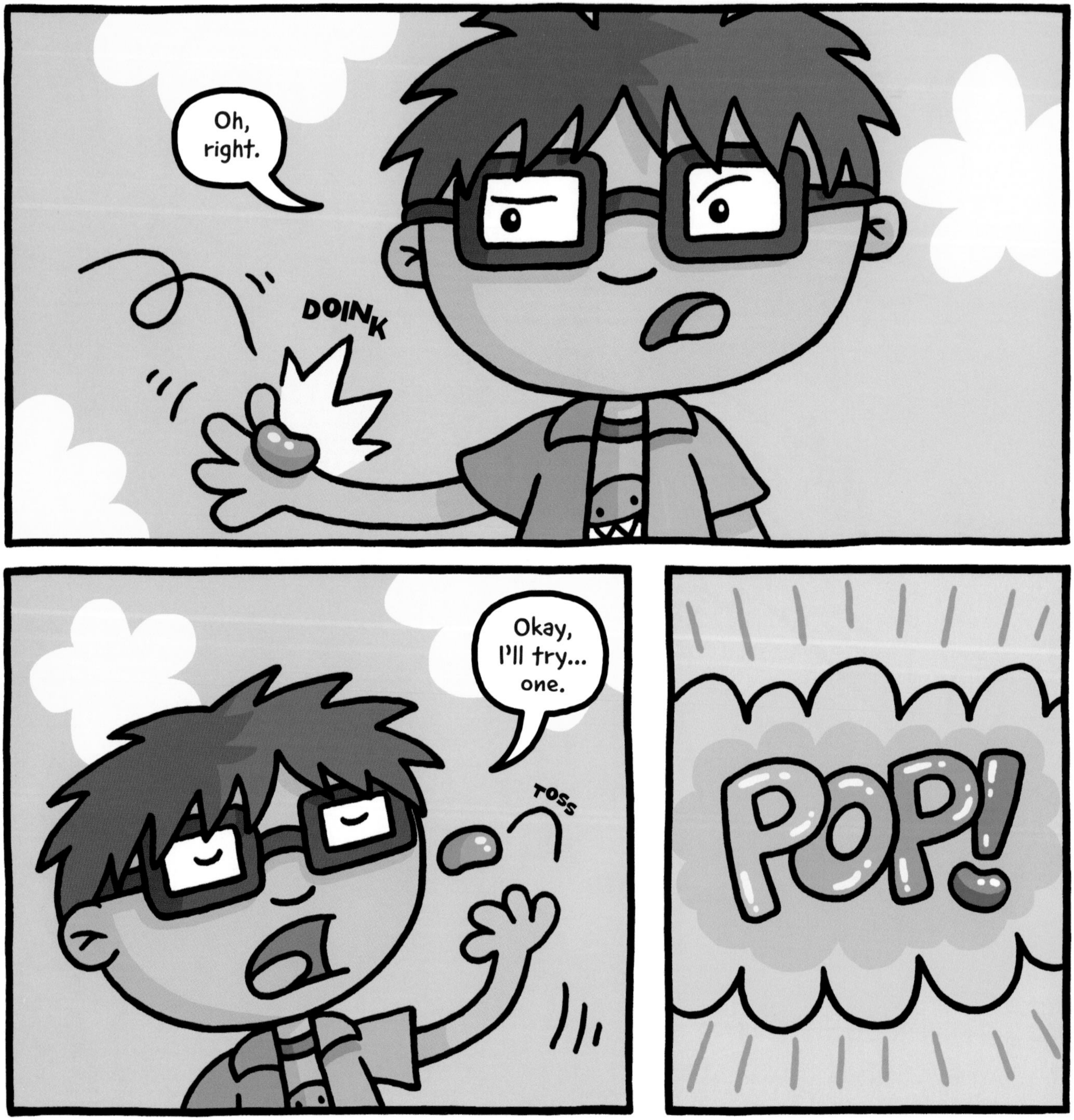
Oh, right.
DOINK
Okay, I'll try... one.
TOSS
POP!

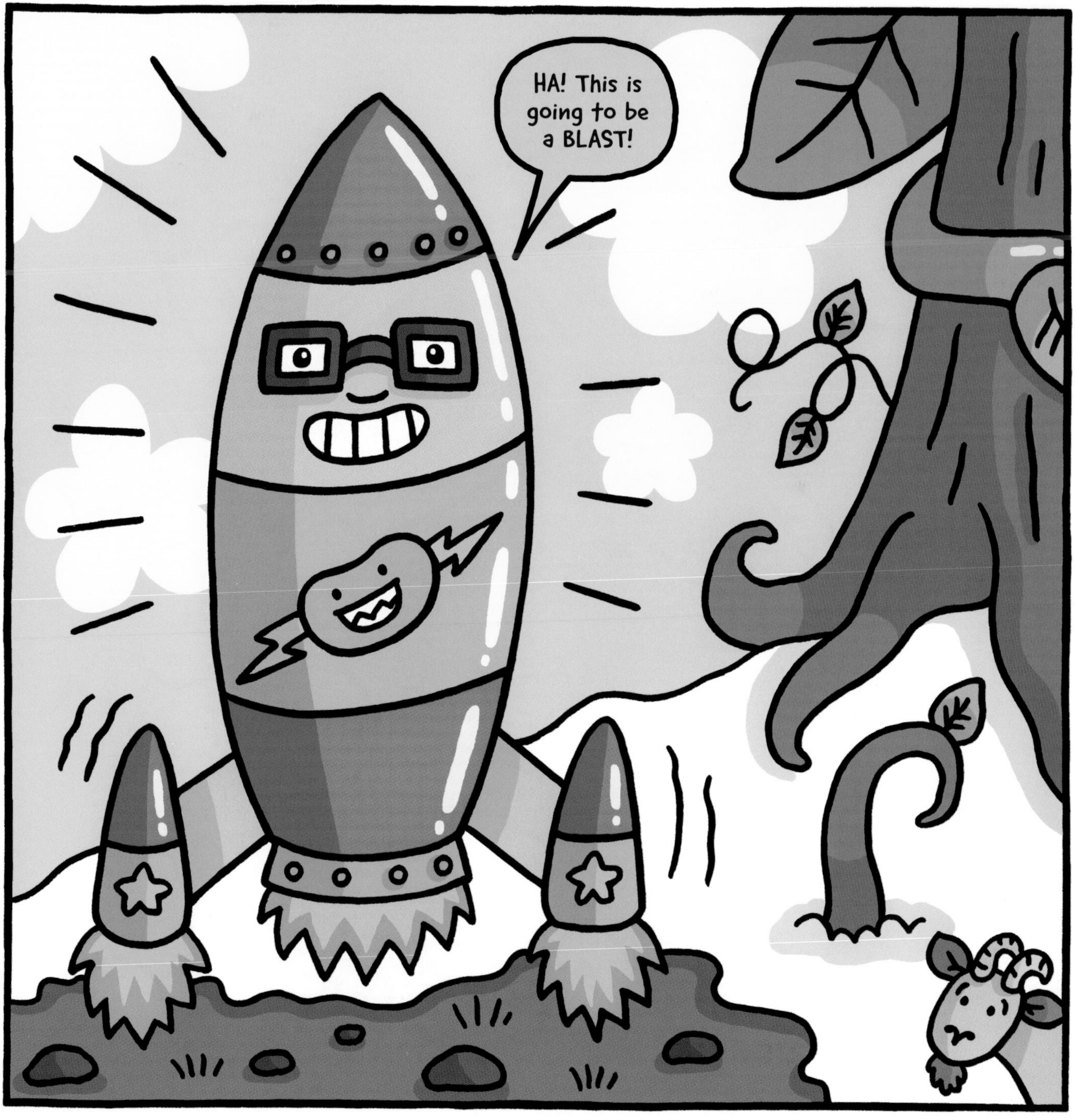
HA! This is going to be a BLAST!

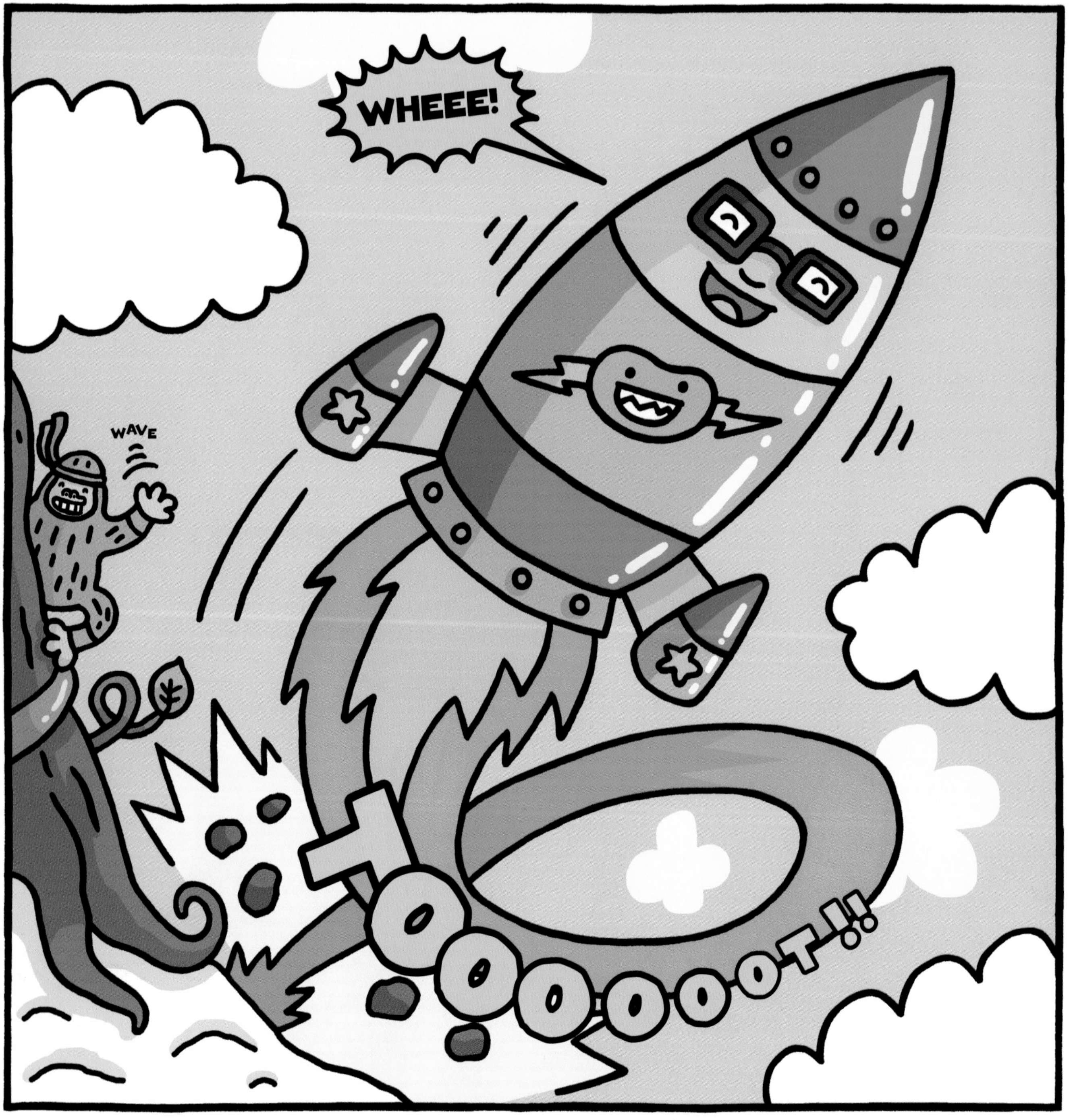
WHEEE!
WAVE
TOOOOOOOT!!

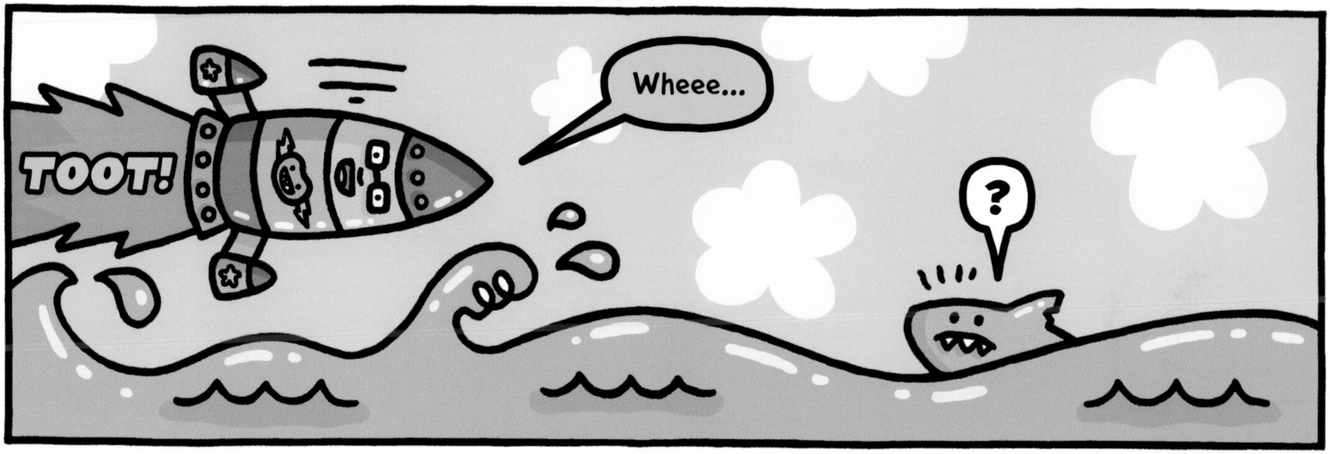
TOOT!
Wheee...
?

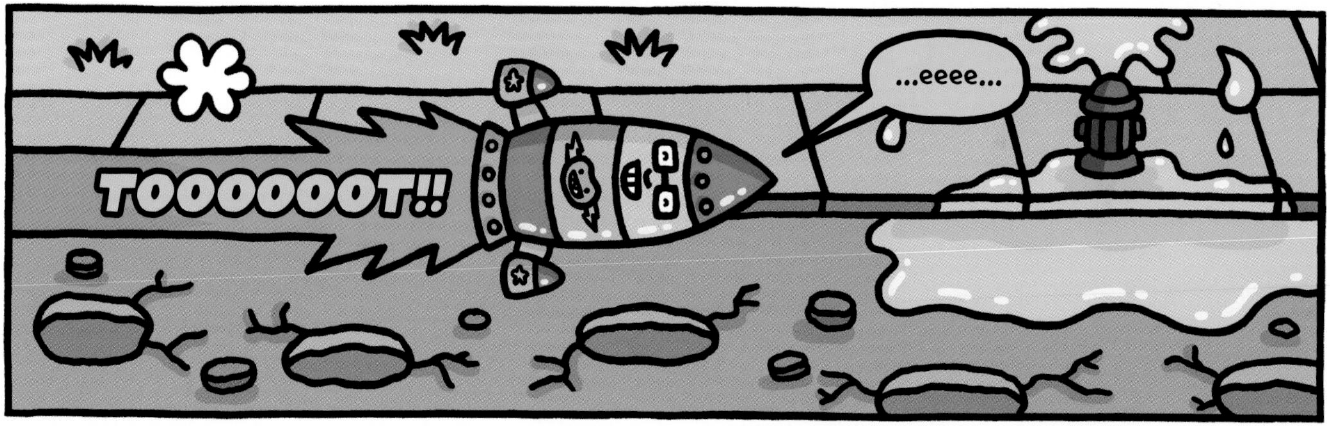
TOOOOOOT!!
...eeee...

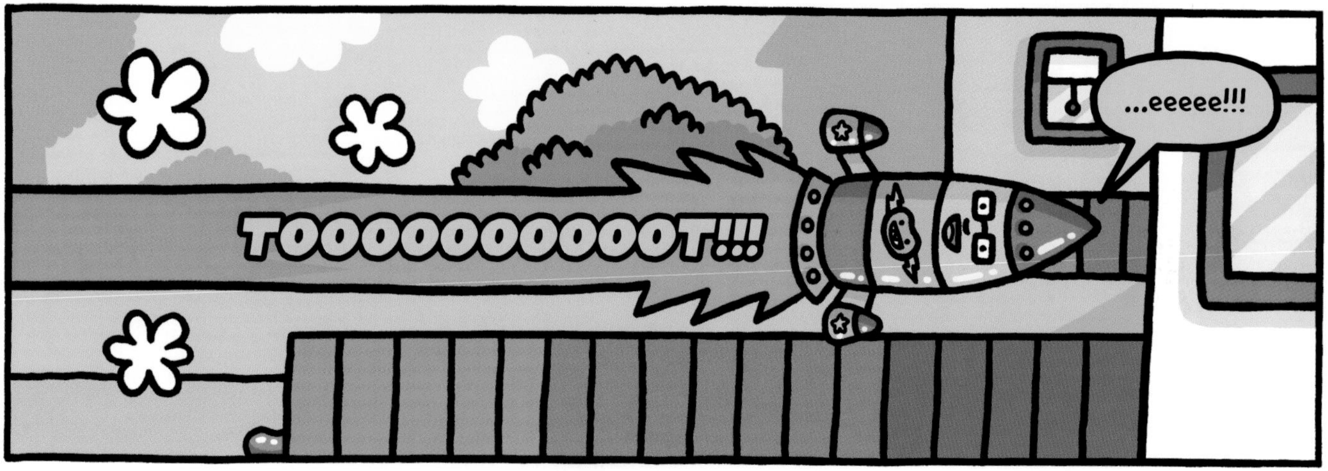
TOOOOOOOOOOOT!!!
...eeeee!!!

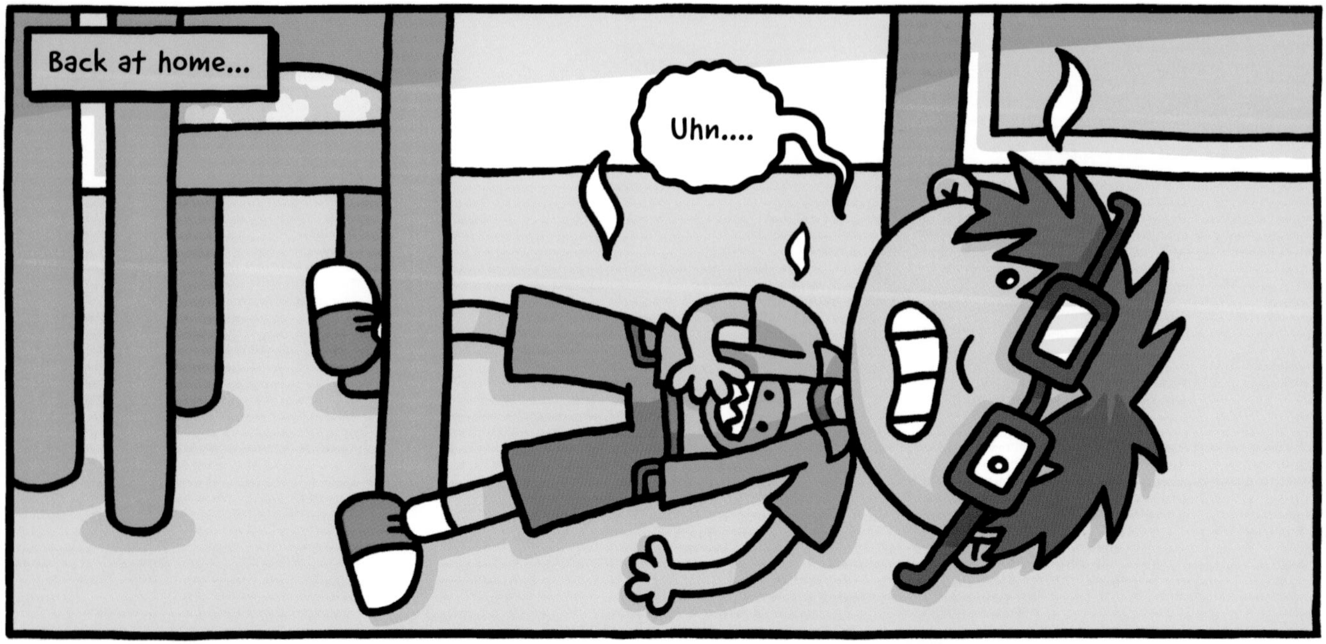
Back at home...
Uhn....

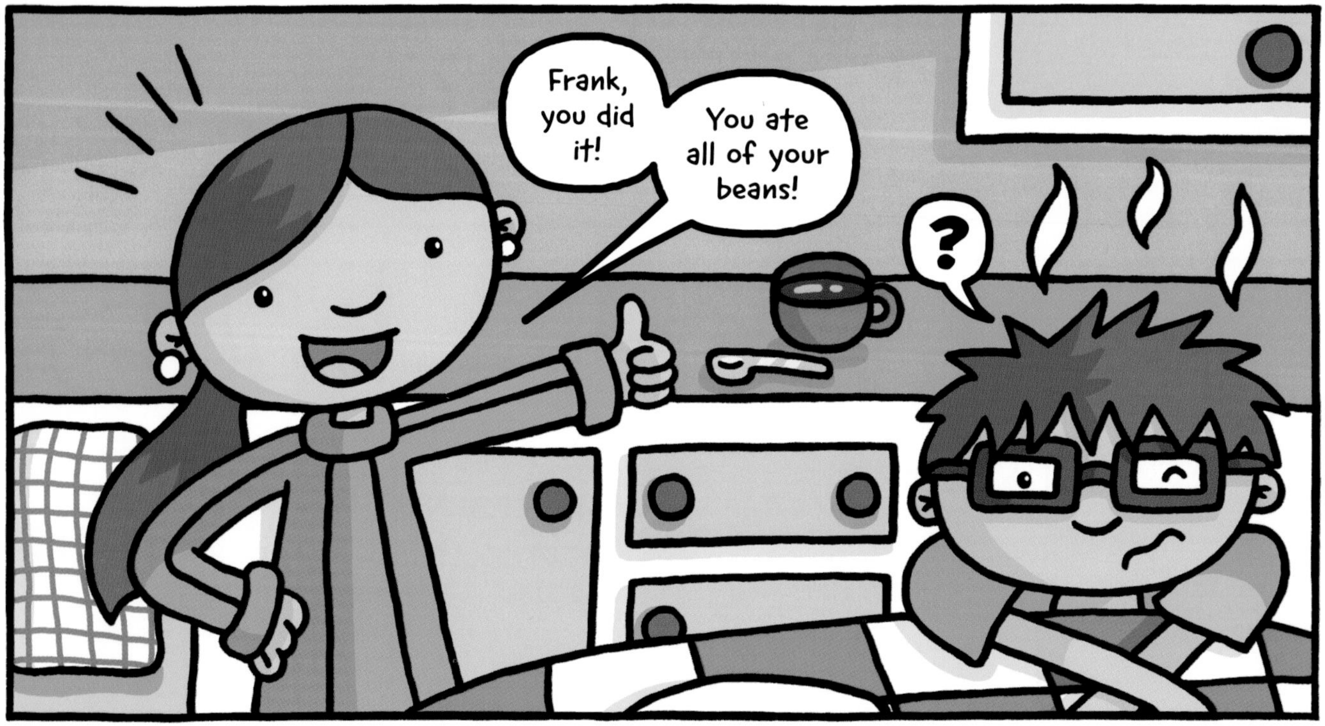
Frank, you did it!
You ate all of your beans!
?

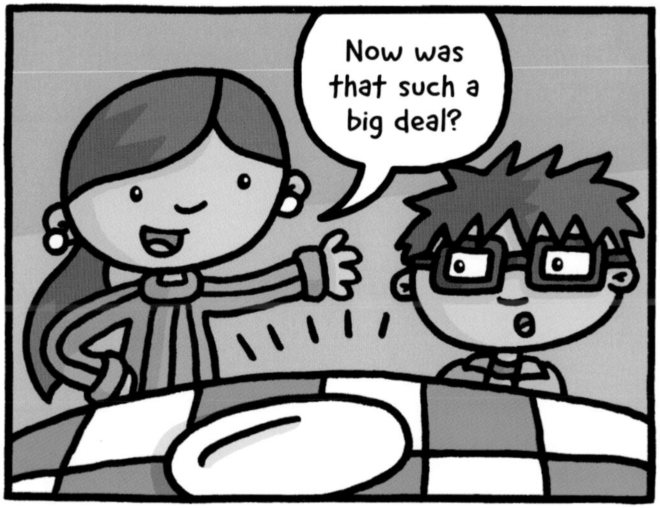
Now was that such a big deal?

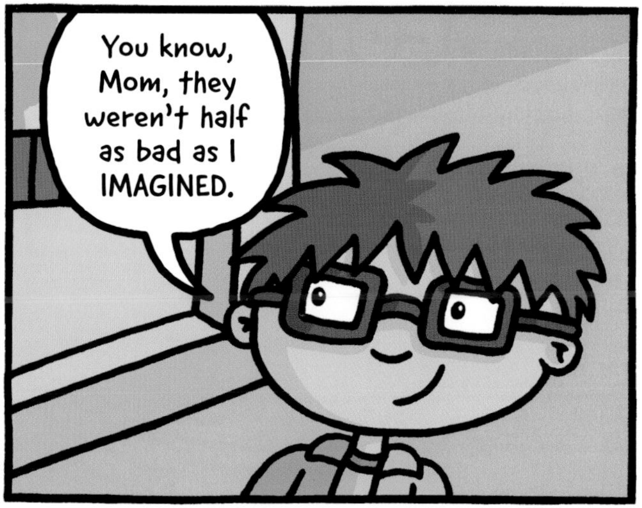
You know, Mom, they weren't half as bad as I IMAGINED.

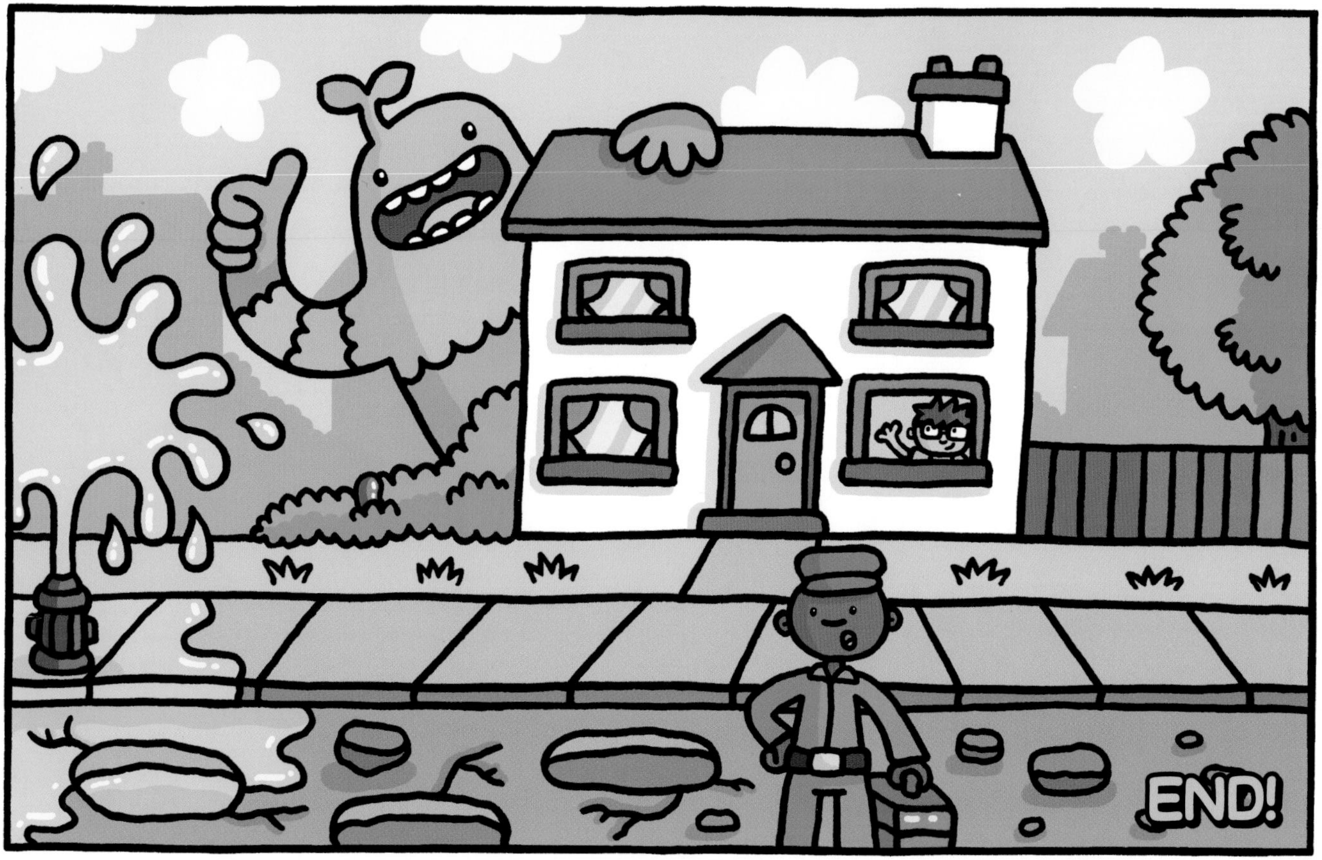
END!

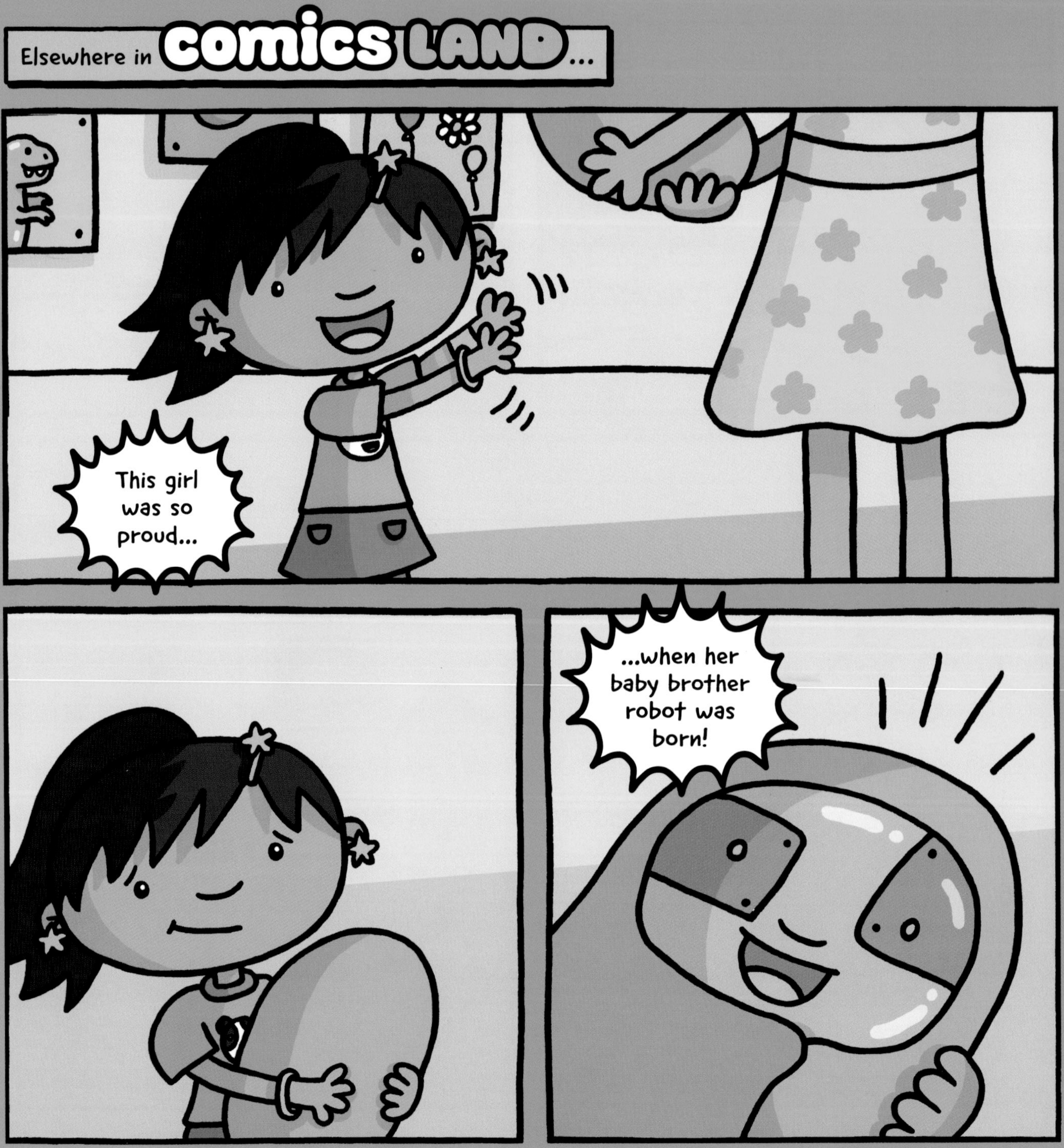
Elsewhere in COMICS LAND...
This girl was so proud...
...when her baby brother robot was born!

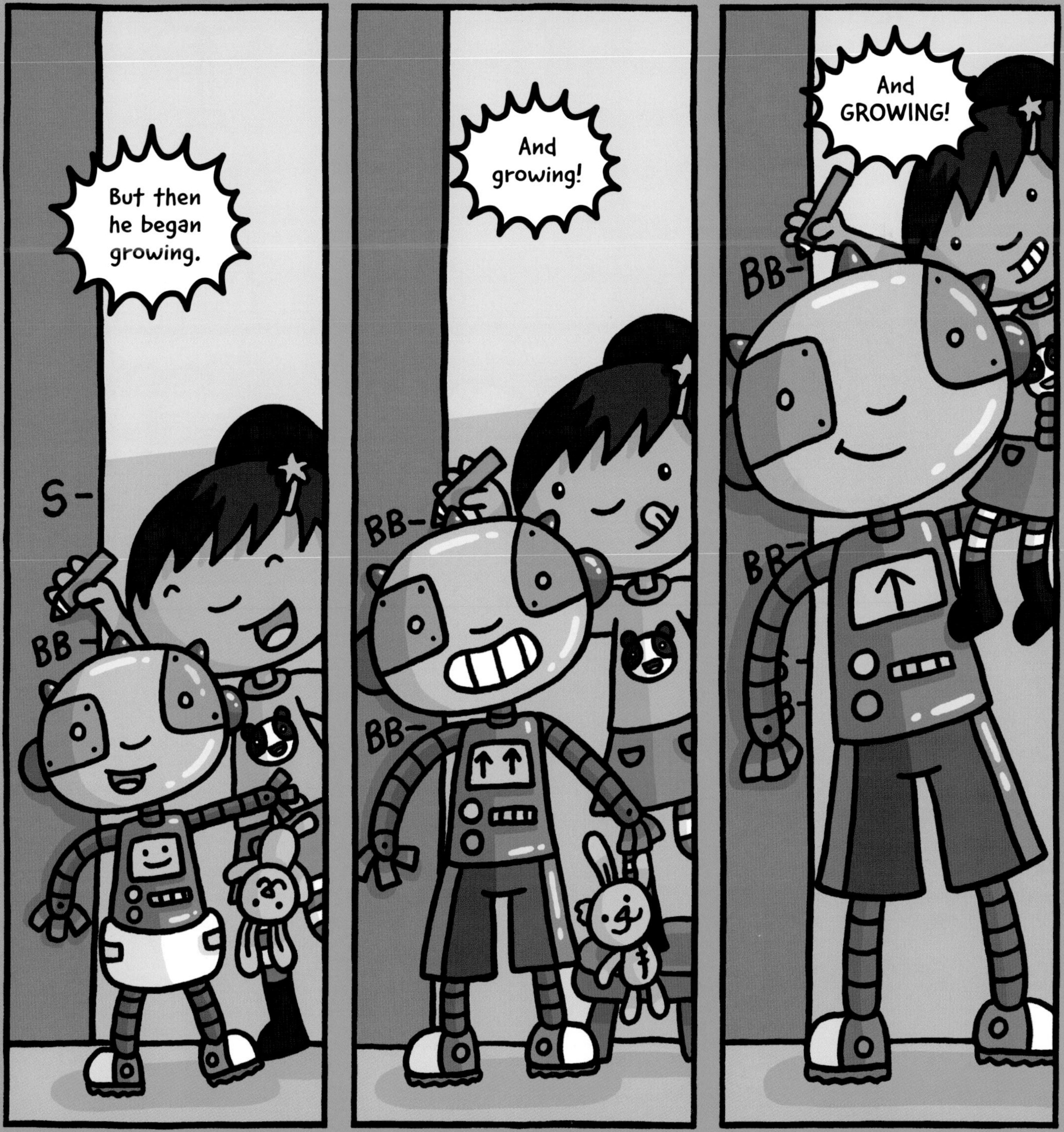
But then he began growing.
S–
BB–
And growing!
BB–
BB–
And GROWING!
BB–
BB–

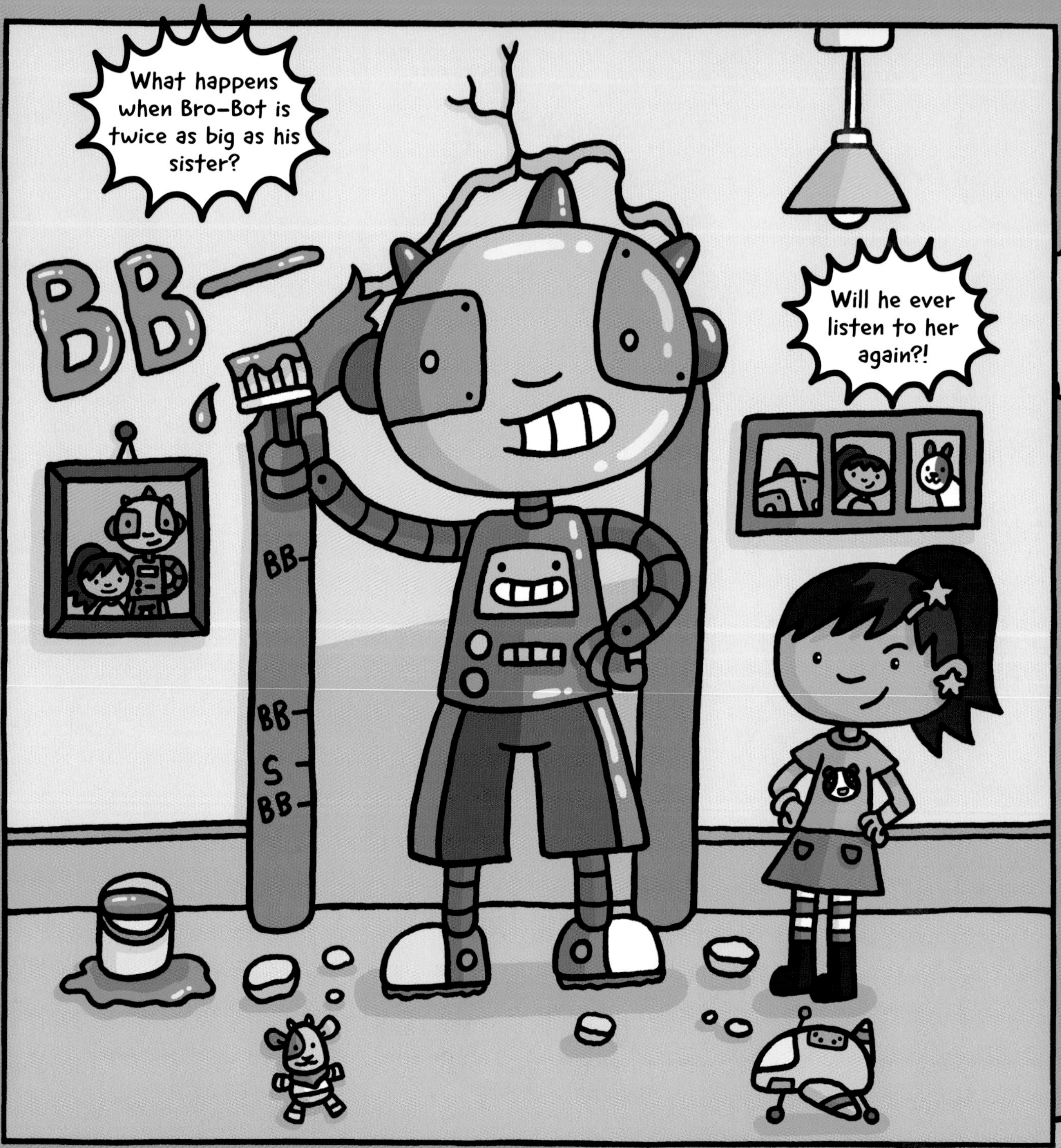
What happens when Bro-Bot is twice as big as his sister?
BB—
Will he ever listen to her again?!
BB-
BB-
S
BB-

Find out in the pages of...

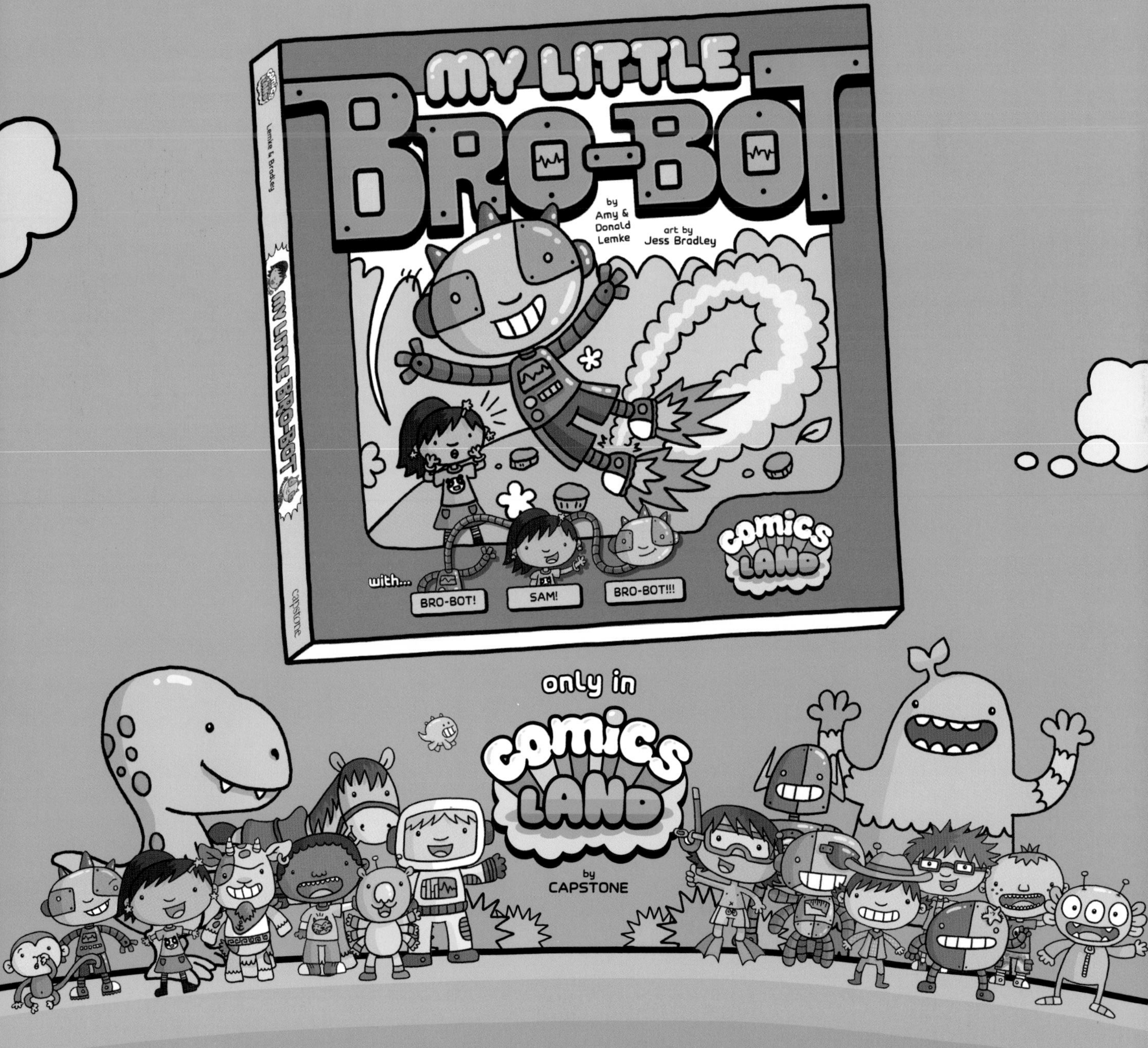
MY LITTLE BRO-BOT
by Amy & Donald Lemke
art by Jess Bradley
Lemke & Bradley
capstone
with...
BRO-BOT!
SAM!
BRO-BOT!!!
COMICS LAND
only in
COMICS LAND
by CAPSTONE

FRANK 'N' BEANS

PRESENTS

GAME TIME!

Every box, balloon, and burst in a comic has a special name and job. Can you match the object with its name?

A. SOUND BURST

B. SURPRISE LINES

C. EXCITEMENT BALLOON

D. WORD BALLOON

E. MOTION LINES

F. SOUND EFFECT

G. NARRATIVE BOX

H. THOUGHT BALLOON

1=D, 2=H, 3=G, 4=A, 5=E, 6=B, 7=F, 8=C

Unscramble the letters to reveal words from the story.

1. ASEBN	5. ANLEKTSBA
2. OSRGS	6. SLABT
3. ROGE	7. EHMO
4. TUNNIAOM	8. GDAMIIEN

1. BEANS, 2. GROSS, 3. OGRE, 4. MOUNTAIN, 5. BEANSTALK, 6. BLAST, 7. HOME, 8. IMAGINED

FIND THE BEANS!

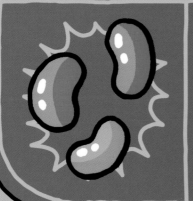

Beans! Beans! They're a magical food! Take another look at the story and search for the special red beans that are hidden throughout the book. There are **10** in all.

FRANK 'N' BEANS PRESENTS

DRAW COMICS!

Want to make your own comic about Frank and Beans? Start by learning to draw the green ogre. Comics Land artist Jess Bradley shows you how in six easy steps!

You will need:

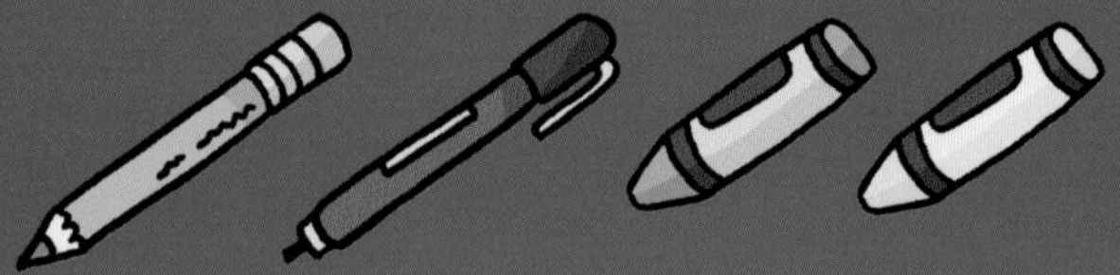

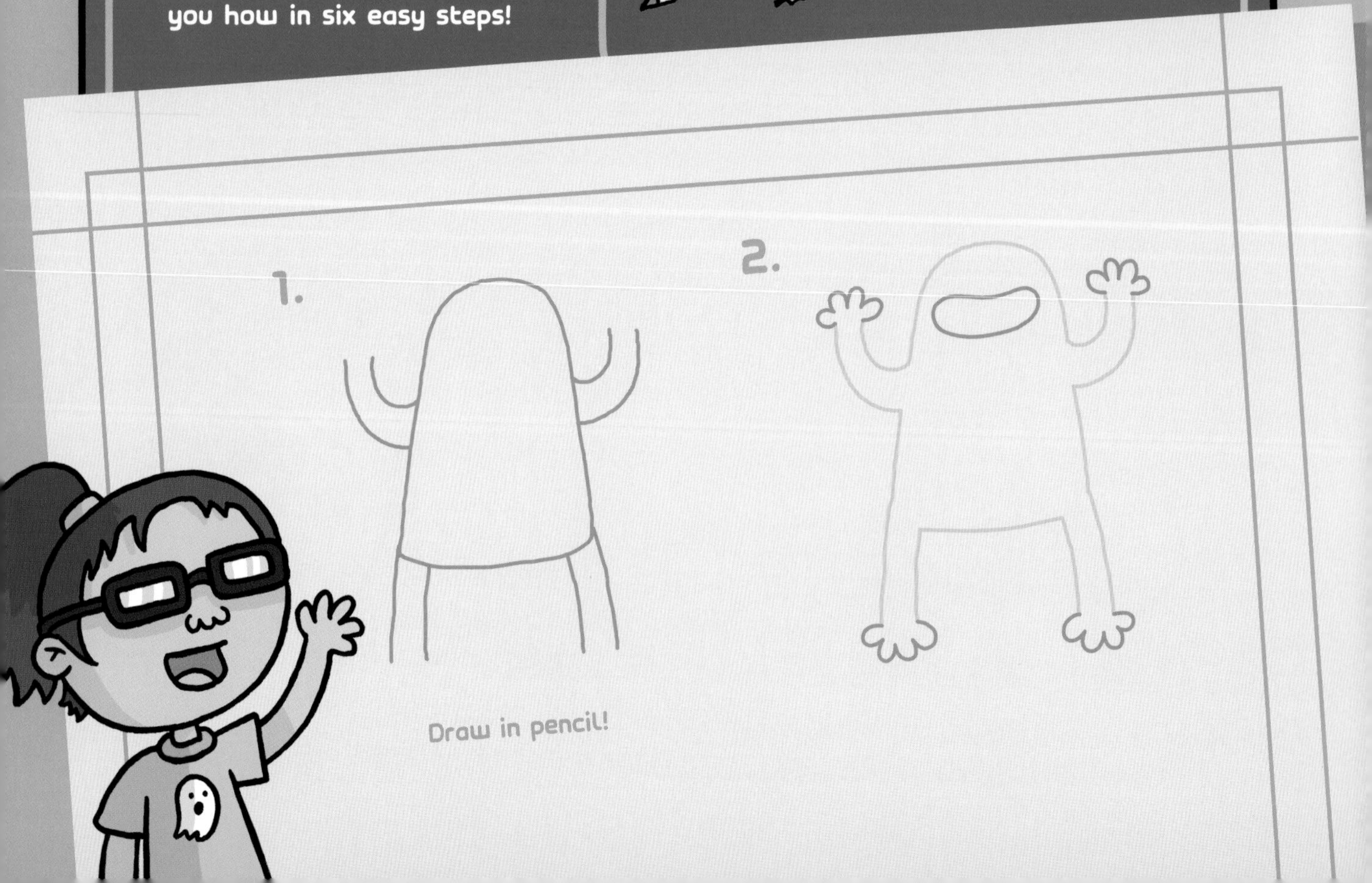
1.
2.
Draw in pencil!

3.

4.

5.

Outline in ink!

6.

Color!

AMY & DONALD LEMKE

AUTHORS

Amy and Donald Lemke are a husband-and-wife team from Hugo, Minnesota. When not caring for their baby girl, fending off their golden retriever, or shooing away their cat, they manage to write a few books. In addition, Donald is a children's book editor and freelance writer, with works published by Capstone, HarperCollins, Running Press, and more. Amy is an Early Childhood Special Education teacher and writer.

JESS BRADLEY

ARTIST

Jess Bradley is an illustrator living and working in Bristol, England. She likes playing video games, painting, and watching bad films. Jess can also be heard to make a high-pitched "squeeeee" when excited, usually while watching videos clips of otters or getting new comics in the mail.

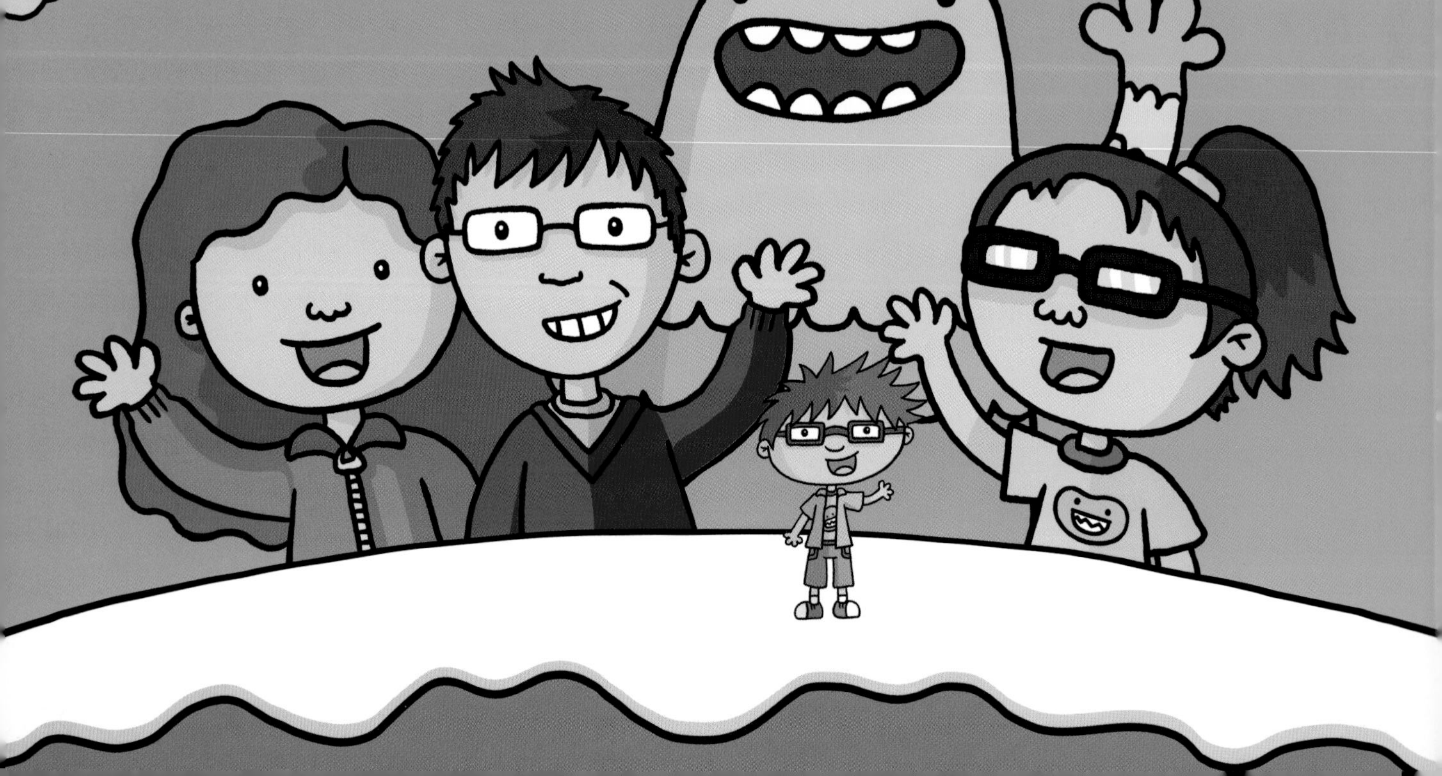

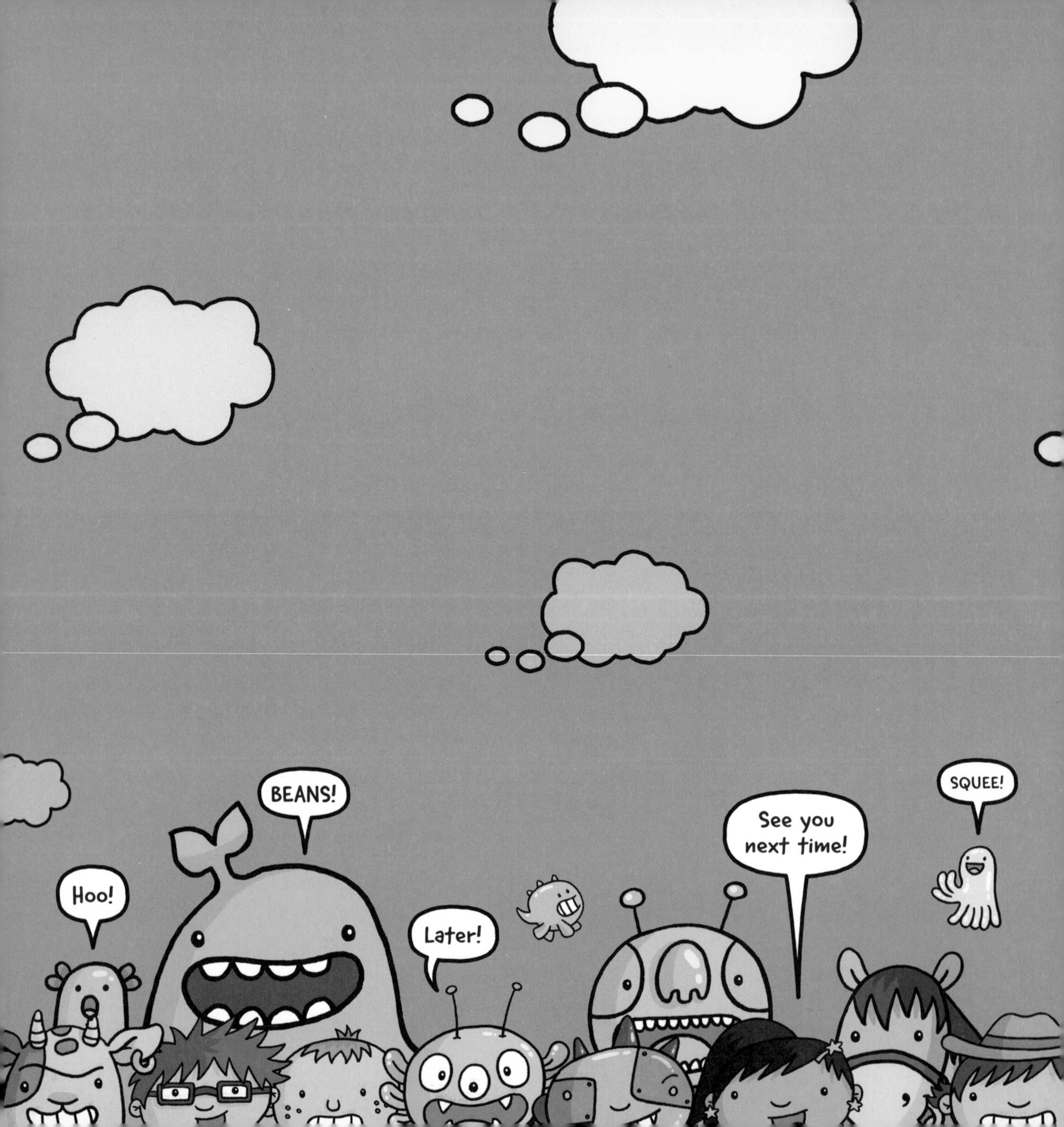
Hoo!
BEANS!
Later!
See you next time!
SQUEE!